# Peeling Potatoes: Katie's Story

BY JAYNE M. BOOTH

Copyright ©2022 by Jayne M. Booth

## Peeling Potatoes: Katie's Story
## Book 1 in the series:
## Rocked in the Cradle of Coal

All rights reserved. No part of this publication may be reproduced, distributed, or transmitted in any form or by any means, including photocopying, recording, or any other electronic or mechanical methods, without the prior written permission of the publisher, except in the case of brief quotations embodied in critical reviews and certain other non-commercial uses permitted by copyright law. Neither the author or the publisher assumes any responsibility or liability whatsoever on behalf of the consumer or reader of this material. Any perceived slight of any individual or organization is purely unintentional.

This book is a fictional historical memoir based on facts obtained through the author's research and written and recorded interviews with people who lived through that era. Some names and characteristics have been changed to protect privacy, some events have been compressed and recreated, and some dialogue has been recreated.

**ISBN: 978-1-7375864-2-5 (eBook)**

**ISBN: 978-1-7375864-3-2 (Paperback)**

**LCCN: 2022906447**

To my Grandmother Anna,

I wish I had told you that you are my hero.

# Acknowledgements

So many people have helped with the creation of this book, and I am thankful for every one of you. Without you these books would have stayed in my head and heart forever. Your help and encouragement are constant blessings in my life.

Christen Booth, who makes cover design and formatting seem effortless, and Danielle Booth, the best ad manager ever – thank you both for your technical skills and for being so easy to work with.

Dave, my husband and number one supporter of whatever I set my mind to, thank you for your patience and understanding in all things, and for picking up the slack when I'm at the end of my rope. Did I mention that I love it when you cook dinner?

To the rest of my tribe who are always ready to encourage and assist with such enthusiasm it leaves me speechless, a heartfelt thank you.

I am supremely thankful to my mother, who will never see this book. She patiently sat with me for countless hours over the years as I interviewed her and recorded her childhood memories. It was so much fun to explore those memories with you, Mom. Thank you to my grandmother and aunts who provided a wealth of information when I, as a child, eavesdropped on their conversations.

A big thank you to other family members, friends, and neighbors who freely shared their memories of life in the early 20th century Northeastern Pennsylvania coal towns.

Historical photos within this book are courtesy of the Photograph Collection of the Luzerne County Historical Society unless otherwise noted.

# Contents

Chapter 1 . . . . . . . . . . . . . . . . . . . . . . . . . . . . . . . . . . .9
Chapter 2 . . . . . . . . . . . . . . . . . . . . . . . . . . . . . . . . . . 15
Chapter 3 . . . . . . . . . . . . . . . . . . . . . . . . . . . . . . . . . . 21
Chapter 4 . . . . . . . . . . . . . . . . . . . . . . . . . . . . . . . . . .27
Chapter 5 . . . . . . . . . . . . . . . . . . . . . . . . . . . . . . . . . .35
Chapter 6 . . . . . . . . . . . . . . . . . . . . . . . . . . . . . . . . . . 41
Chapter 7 . . . . . . . . . . . . . . . . . . . . . . . . . . . . . . . . . .49
Chapter 8 . . . . . . . . . . . . . . . . . . . . . . . . . . . . . . . . . .53
Chapter 9 . . . . . . . . . . . . . . . . . . . . . . . . . . . . . . . . . .63
Chapter 10 . . . . . . . . . . . . . . . . . . . . . . . . . . . . . . . . .69
Chapter 11. . . . . . . . . . . . . . . . . . . . . . . . . . . . . . . . . .75
Chapter 12 . . . . . . . . . . . . . . . . . . . . . . . . . . . . . . . . .83
Chapter 13 . . . . . . . . . . . . . . . . . . . . . . . . . . . . . . . . .99
Chapter 14 . . . . . . . . . . . . . . . . . . . . . . . . . . . . . . . .105
Chapter 15 . . . . . . . . . . . . . . . . . . . . . . . . . . . . . . . . 111
Glossary . . . . . . . . . . . . . . . . . . . . . . . . . . . . . . . . . 119
About the Author . . . . . . . . . . . . . . . . . . . . . . . . . .122

A NOTE FROM THE AUTHOR BEFORE YOU READ
"ROCKED IN THE CRADLE OF COAL" BOOKS

What was life like in the early 1900s for a poor eastern European immigrant seeking a better life in America? If you had only a meager education and didn't speak English well, if you had spent most of your savings buying passage on a ship to The Land of Opportunity, and if you also had a family to support, then a job in the Pennsylvania coal mines was your best chance at achieving The American Dream.

Can you imagine long days working hundreds of feet underground in cold dampness? There was no light except for a small carbide lamp bracketed above the brim of your canvas cap. Water was constantly dripping down the black mine walls, and the rocky floor was wet and slippery. Sticky black coal dust filled the air and coated your skin, clothing, and lungs.

Many miners got sick from inhaling the coal dust. Miners Asthma, or Black Lung Disease, forced some miners to leave the mines. Deadly mining accidents claimed others. If a miner was not able to work, then his family no longer received his pay. They also had to vacate their company-owned house, unless one of his boys was old enough to work in the mine. That is why sons of miners often had to quit school early, even before completing elementary school, so they could help support their family.

Young girls also learned to contribute to the success of their family. They helped with cooking and household chores, gardening, and tending younger siblings. Eventually, even the girls left school early to work outside the home for whatever meager pay they could earn. Did the children get to keep their wages? No, children dutifully handed over their pay envelopes to their parents. Survival of the family was everyone's primary concern.

As you read, "ROCKED IN THE CRADLE OF COAL" books you will notice that some words are printed in bold type. Those words are defined in the Glossary at the end of the book.

I hope you enjoy this trip back in time.

Jayne M. Booth
author

# Chapter 1

Five-year-old Katie lay in bed watching Mama knead the bread dough. Punch, punch, fold, and punch. Mama paused to brush a strand of pale blonde hair from her forehead with the back of one floury hand. She noticed Katie watching her.

"Why are you not asleep, Little One?" Mama asked. "See, your sisters and brother are all fast asleep. It is late."

Katie turned her head and saw her sleeping sisters beside her—ten-year-old Tillie was closest, and eleven-year-old Mary was on Tillie's other side. The three girls were all lying crosswise on the big double bed, a warm fluffy feather tick pulled up to their chins. Katie glanced across the room where her seven-year-old brother, Wasyl, was softly snoring on his little cot.

"Mama, I wonder what school will be like," Katie whispered.

"Well, in Old Country girls didn't go to school—except for the very rich, so I only know what I have been told," said Mama. "But I do know that there will be many other children there, and you will make new friends. You will learn how to read and write. It will be fun to learn something new every day, don't you think?"

"Tillie says they only speak English in school. I hardly know any English. Why don't they speak Russian like we do here at home, Mama?"

Mama sighed. "Katie, this is America. You are an American. You must speak the language of your country—yes?"

"Yes, Mama," Katie agreed. "Mama?"

"What now?"

"Are you an American?"

"Not yet, but someday..."

Katie bit her lip. "What should I say if the teacher asks how old I am? Will she send me home if I say five? Should I say six?"

Mama considered for a moment, then said, "Katie, we must always tell the truth. The Lord knows that I need to work. He knows that you can't stay home alone. I have prayed about this. God has provided a job for me—now we must trust Him."

Mama went back to kneading the dough. Punch, punch, fold, and punch. Katie listened to the rhythmic sound of Mama's hands pounding the dough and slowly drifted off to sleep.

***

"Katie! Katie! Wake up or you'll be late for your first day of school," Tillie whispered in her little sister's ear.

Katie sat up and rubbed her eyes. She smelled coffee simmering on the black coal stove.

"Hurry!" said Mary. "You may wear your Sunday dress for the first day." She held up the light green dress that Mama had made for Katie just last spring.

Katie slid to the floor. She ran over to the water pipe and filled the chipped white enamel basin. Then she splashed cold water on her face and dried it on the thin towel Mama kept by the sink. She skipped back to Mary, who helped her squirm into the green dress that Katie loved so much. Mary helped her button the buttons Katie couldn't reach and combed her little sister's short hair and straight bangs.

"There you go. All finished," said Mary.

Katie went to look in the small mirror on the wall over the basin. Large, pale-green eyes stared back at her. Mama said that Katie's Sunday dress matched her eyes, and that made Katie happy. She did not like her mousey brown hair at all, though. It wasn't soft and silvery blonde like Mama's and Tillie's. It wasn't even sandy blonde like Mary's thick long hair that she wore in four shiny buns around the base of her head. Nor was Katie's hair the lustrous deep brown shade belonging to Ann, her oldest sister. Mama said that Ann got her glossy brown hair from Papa. Katie envied Ann's long braids, which reached almost to her waist.

Mama had given up on Katie's thin, wispy hair. Neither blonde nor brown, and too skimpy for braids, Mama had finally cut Katie's hair straight across, even with her chin, and with a fringe of short straight bangs.

"You look like a boy, Onion Eyes," teased Wasyl behind her. "A boy in a dress!"

"Stop it!" Katie yelled at him.

"Onion Eyes! Onion Eyes!" said Wasyl softly, so Mama wouldn't hear. But, as usual, Mama heard him anyway.

"Wasyl, I believe it is time to feed Prince," said Mama, thrusting a bowl containing a few scraps of the boarders' leftover breakfast into his hands. The black German Shepherd, who had been napping near the coal stove, roused at the sound of his name. He loped, tail swinging, toward the door. Wasyl said no more and went out to the back stoop to fill Prince's dish and give him fresh water for the day.

Katie turned tearful eyes toward her mother. "Mama..." she started.

"No, Little One, you do not look like a boy. And see, I have a green ribbon for your hair. You will look as nice as any other girl in the first grade." Mama tied the ribbon under Katie's hair with the bow on top of her head. "There now, sit down and eat. It is a long walk to school."

Mama had fixed Katie's favorite breakfast: a thick slice of warm buttered bread—no wretched egg this morning. Mama raised chickens in the backyard. Katie liked the chickens. She played with them and even gave them names, but Katie could never choke down even half of an egg. And when Mama made chicken for supper, Katie couldn't eat at all, because she knew which chicken it was.

Mama poured strong dark coffee into Katie's mug, filling it halfway. Then she added rich cream to the top. She sprinkled a spoonful of sugar in, then winked at Katie and quickly added another without anyone else noticing. Katie gave her mother a small, grateful smile. Her first day of school would be all right. She just knew it.

# Chapter 2

Central School was all the way uptown. It was a two-story brick building and contained classes for first through sixth grades. As they crossed the schoolyard, Mary and Tillie waved to friends they knew from last year, but Katie didn't know anyone. She stared at all the strange faces as they passed through the noisy crowd of children. Tillie ran off to join a group of girls. Katie reached for Mary's hand. Everyone seemed to be laughing and calling out to others, but no one talked to Katie.

She followed her sister up the wide steps and into the large brick building. The first classroom on the left was for the first and second grades. Katie sat in the seat Mary showed her in the front row. Mary whispered, "Just say that you're six." Then she said goodbye and went to her own classroom upstairs.

Katie glanced around the room. There were five rows of children's desks. In front was the teacher's desk and chair. A long blackboard lined the wall behind it. Above the blackboard were cards with printed letters and numbers on them. Some of the letters Katie knew, because Tillie had taught her how to spell her name in English and how to write the numbers one to ten.

A big American flag hung above the letter and number cards, directly behind the teacher's chair. To the right of the flag, on a nail, hung a long wooden paddle. Katie had heard stories about this particular paddle from her sisters. In fact, one time last year, Wasyl had gotten paddled in front of the whole class for arriving late to school for the second time. It was a shame, Mama had said, a disgrace on the family, and she had switched him again with a thin branch from the peach tree. Katie squeezed her eyes shut and hoped she would never get paddled at school.

Just then the school bell rang, and all the other children began to file in from the schoolyard. Last of all, a trim young woman entered and closed the door behind her. The children immediately found a seat, first grade in the front and second grade behind them. The teacher walked briskly toward her desk, her shoes tap, tap, tapping across the wooden floor. She was young and had a kind face. Katie thought she was pretty.

"Good morning, class," said the teacher.

"Good morning, Teacher," the older students responded in unison.

The teacher turned to the blackboard and printed in large letters: MISS WINT. She repeated it slowly for the class.

"That is my name," said Miss Wint. "Now I would like to meet you. Some I remember from last year. Welcome back, second graders! But I see we have several new students. Would the new first graders please stand?"

Katie stood with eleven other children. She studied them as, one by one, the children went to the teacher, stated their names, and answered each question she asked. Katie noticed that the other first graders were all taller than she was. A couple of them did not speak English very well. Katie felt relieved at that. She wondered if Miss Wint would guess that she really was not old enough to be in first grade. Finally, the teacher nodded in Katie's direction. Katie stepped forward.

"And what is your name?" Miss Wint asked with a smile.

"Kathryn Swistovich, but I am called Katie," Katie answered.

"Are you Wasyl's sister?"

"Yes."

"How old are you, Katie?"

Katie looked down. She knew she needed to tell the truth. Mama would want her to do that. Would Miss Wint let her stay? She just had to.

"Katie, how old are you?" repeated Miss Wint.

"Five," Katie said softly.

Miss Wint thought for a moment, then said, "Wasyl, please come up to my desk."

Wasyl walked from the back of the classroom and nudged Katie closer to the teacher's desk. Miss Wint sat in her chair and faced both children. She whispered, "Wasyl, your sister is not old enough to be in school. You have my permission to take her home to your mother. Then you may return to class."

"But Miss Wint, Mama isn't home. She got a job working on **The Flats** during the day. Since Papa died, Mama has kept boarders, but it's not enough money. She must work, Miss Wint. That's why Mama sent Katie to school—to be safe – so that Mama would be able to work."

Miss Wint's forehead wrinkled as she thought some more.

"Katie is smart," added Wasyl. "She can spell her name—and count. Do it, Katie," he ordered.

Katie stood up straight and obeyed. "One, two, three, four, five, six, seven, eight, nine, ten," she recited.

"Very nice!" said Miss Wint. "And can you spell your name?"

Katie walked to the blackboard and picked up a piece of chalk. "KATIE" she printed as neatly as she could.

"I'm impressed," said the teacher, her eyes twinkling. She put an arm around Katie's shoulders and whispered, "Very well, you may stay in the first grade. It will be our little secret." In a louder voice, she said, "Thank you, children. You may all be seated."

Then Miss Wint picked up a large black Bible from her desk and read a short scripture. Katie didn't understand much of it because it was in English, but the lilting words sounded beautiful. After that, the children bowed their heads, and together with their teacher, they recited the Lord's Prayer. Katie knew this in Russian, so she thought it wouldn't be too hard to learn it in English.

Finally, the class stood to say the Pledge of Allegiance to the flag. Katie didn't understand that either, but she knew it must be important, because following their teacher's lead, everyone stood straight and tall next to their desks, right hand over their hearts, eyes on the flag at the front of the room. Katie also stood with her hand over her heart, but she just listened this time. She decided that she would ask Tillie to teach her the pledge at home.

After the opening exercises were completed, it was time to start learning. Katie could hardly wait. Miss Wint gave each child a whole tablet and a brand-new pencil. A tablet and a pencil! Katie had never had her very own tablet and pencil before. She decided that she would not waste a single sheet of paper, and that she would never, ever lose her pencil.

At recess, Tillie and Mary sighed with relief to hear that Katie was allowed to stay in school.

"Won't Mama be happy!" exclaimed Tillie.

"Yes." Mary smiled. "And next year, when I'm twelve, I can join Ann doing housework. Then we will be rich!"

## Chapter 3

Now that Katie was officially enrolled in school, no one had to wake her in the morning. She couldn't wait for each new day to begin. The five o'clock train, which ran right past the rickety backyard fence, usually rumbled her awake even before Mama started to make breakfast.

She hadn't worn her Sunday dress to school since the first day. Now she wore her everyday dress. It was gray with a pleated bodice and a round white collar. Katie didn't like this one nearly as much as the pale green dress that matched her eyes, but she understood that her Sunday dress was only for special occasions.

Every day as Katie and her sisters walked to school, Katie's new friend, Adeline Adams, joined them halfway. Adeline was also in the first grade. Her parents owned a tavern uptown and were always busy with their customers. Adeline had no brothers or sisters, so the finely furnished apartment above their tavern was lonely for her. Sometimes she came to Katie's house after school.

Mama always expected the girls to start supper for the family and the boarders before she came home from work. Mary was in charge. The first thing she did was hand Wasyl the empty coal bucket to fill with coal to heat the stove. He could find good coal down by the railroad tracks or on the **culm** banks, where waste coal and slate piled up around the mines, if he didn't stop to play with one of his friends instead. Piece by piece, he would fill the bucket to the brim. He feared Mama's wrath even more than the paddle at school, so he always brought the full bucket home well before supper time. Then he could play until supper was ready.

Katie's job was peeling the potatoes because that was easy, and because it kept her out of Mary's way. Katie hated to see that huge basin full of potatoes plunked down in front of her every afternoon. Mama, the children, and the four boarders ate a lot of potatoes!

The first time Adeline came to Katie's house after school, Katie thought her friend wouldn't like it there. She knew that the basement of the wood-frame house she shared with her mother and siblings was not as pretty as Adeline's apartment above the tavern. There were no fine rugs on the floor, only rag carpets that **Titka** (Aunt) Catherine had given to Mama when she replaced hers with new carpets. But they were clean, if worn, and Mama said that was all that mattered.

At home, Adeline had a room all to herself and several dolls she had shown to Katie. Her dolls had clothes to change and even tiny high-buttoned shoes. Katie didn't have any dolls and shared a bed in the kitchen with her two sisters.

Katie noticed other differences, too. Adeline wore a different dress to school every day of the week, and they were so pretty. Even her petticoat and bloomers were trimmed in lace. Although Mama always made sure her girls had clean, serviceable clothes, they weren't fancy. Their underwear was sewn from bleached flour sacks. Cooking and baking for the family and the boarders who lived upstairs provided plenty of flour sacks that could be fashioned into free underwear for the children. Mama was wise and thrifty, and Katie respected that, but still... bloomers trimmed with lace would be nice.

As much as Katie hated to peel potatoes, Adeline seemed to love doing that chore. This perplexed Katie, but sharing that job with her friend made it much more enjoyable than doing it alone. Mary didn't mind, as long as they didn't spend more time talking and giggling than working. Once Adeline learned how to manage the paring knife, they finished with the potatoes in half the time and could go outside and play on the back porch out of Mary's way.

As the days grew cooler and shorter, and the leaves on the trees turned to gold, orange, and red, Adeline came home with Katie more and more often after school. Adeline had confided that she didn't like to be alone in the apartment after dark while her mother and father waited on customers downstairs until late in the evening.

"Katie," Mary said one morning before they reached the spot where Adeline was waiting for them, "you must not invite Adeline to come home with you every day after school. It is starting to get dark earlier now, and she will soon be too afraid to walk home at five o'clock."

"I could walk her uptown," said Katie. As she hurried to keep up with her older sisters her words made little puffs of steam in the nippy morning air.

"You!" said Tillie, her blue eyes wide in disbelief.

"You're too afraid to walk the path to the outhouse alone in the dark."

"That's right," Mary wisely agreed. "After you walked Adeline home, who would walk you back home?"

Katie thought about this, and she knew her sisters were correct. But poor Adeline, all by herself in the silent apartment—playing with no one except her toys. Alone with no one to talk to... "Mary, I feel sorry for her," Katie explained, twisting her mouth. "Adeline needs to come to our house after school."

"Needs? What do we have that Adeline could possibly need? It seems to me that she already has plenty of everything."

Tillie rolled her eyes and nodded in agreement. The girls had often admired Adeline's pretty clothes. Mama had taught them to always be thankful for what they had—"There are others worse off," she would say—and not to be envious of others. Still, it was hard not to notice.

"She needs us," Katie persisted. "She needs someone to talk to and laugh with. She hates to be home alone with only her dolls for company. She needs to peel potatoes with me."

"Peel potatoes?" Mary and Tillie both repeated.

"Adeline told me that if I let her help peel potatoes after school every day that she would take me to the picture show on Saturday. Her father gives her ten cents every Saturday, and that is enough for both of us to go to the Nickelette."

Tillie and Mary stared, open-mouthed, first at Katie, then at each other.

Mary was the first to speak. "Maybe we can take turns helping Katie walk Adeline home."

Katie smiled hopefully. At last, Mary understood.

"I can't believe it," Tillie said over and over. "I just can't believe it. She needs to peel potatoes."

## Chapter 4

Katie was proud of her progress in first grade. She was good at memorizing, so she could recite the Pledge of Allegiance with the rest of the class now and was learning to speak English. Miss Wint taught the class that each letter of the alphabet made certain sounds, and soon Katie could put the sounds together to make words. She could even recognize simple words outside her **primer**. Words like GO, THE, OF, STOP, CAT, and DOG seemed to jump out at her from signs, newspapers, and labels. She could tell that Miss Wint was relieved that Katie had no trouble keeping up with the other first-grade students.

Mama was also relieved. With Katie safely enrolled in school, Mama could work all day on the farms on The Flats, the low-lying fields bordering the Susquehanna River banks. While the weather was warm, Mama helped pick tomatoes and green beans, but now that autumn was here cabbage, pumpkins, and squash were the main crops. Mama worked hard every day. She didn't make much money, but her boss was kind to the immigrants who worked for him. He allowed them to take home any vegetables they could carry in their lunch buckets at the end of the day. These vegetables helped to supplement the vegetables Mama grew in her small home garden.

Added to Mama's **pierogies**, **halushki**, and rich soups with homemade noodles or dumplings and fresh baked bread, no one in the house went to bed hungry. Meat was an occasional treat for the boarders, but the family only ate meat on holidays, which was just fine with Katie, who loved animals and had figured out where all meat comes from.

Mama was known among the miners for her simple but delicious home cooking. It wasn't fancy, but it was enough. She was choosy about her boarders and insisted that anyone boarding in her house be clean and employed full-time. Mama wouldn't accept anyone without a recommendation from someone she knew and respected. A recommendation from the parish priest was the best.

As a landlady, she laid out a few house rules she expected all her boarders to follow. Katie remembered one boarder who had crossed Mama's line of tolerance. One night, this particular man had come home drunk after 9:00 p.m.—the time Mama locked all the doors for the night. His heavy banging on the front door had awakened the children. For a long time, they'd listened to the staggering man begging to be let in.

"You know, these doors are locked at nine o'clock sharp, no excuses!" Mama said through the closed door.

"Aw, Missus! I just wanted a little drink with my friends," he slurred.

"There be no drunkards in this house, and you not be the first. Tonight, you sleep outside!" Mama declared in her broken English.

With that, Mama went to bed. The dejected boarder

finally curled up on the porch and sang himself to sleep. The next morning, he awoke to find his belongings in a neat bundle next to him, and he was never allowed in the house again. Word of this man's fate got around, and the other boarders, thankful for their clean but humble surroundings, never jeopardized their status by breaking Mama's rules.

After a good supper, the boarders liked to sit on the porch if the evening wasn't too cool and talk about the Old Country, the land they had left to come to America. On these occasions, Katie and her sisters hurried to clean up the kitchen after supper, while Mama worked on her mending or started another batch of bread dough for the next day.

While Mary and Tillie finished washing the dishes in the big basin, Wasyl shook out the rag rugs over the porch railing and fed Prince, and Katie swept the kitchen floor. When they were finished, the girls crept outside to listen quietly as the men spun their tales.

Katie sat on the edge of the porch petting Prince, so she wouldn't miss a single word. Katie liked to hear about life in other countries, but she thought the ghost stories were best. Forgetting about petting the dog, she sat wide-eyed with fright as each man tried to outdo the last one with an even spookier tale. Katie shivered as the evening breeze tousled her short, wispy hair. She wrapped her arms around her body and looked warily over her shoulder.

"Boo!" She gasped, not expecting to see anyone there. Wasyl had crept up unnoticed and stood in the yard beside the porch, peering through the banister close to Katie.

"That means a ghost just passed you," he whispered.

"What?" she asked, trying to appear brave.

"That's why you shivered. It was a ghost passing by, right behind you. That's what they say, you know."

Katie gulped. Mary turned to them for a moment. "Oh, Wasyl, stop teasing her," she scolded softly, and turned her attention back to the story in progress.

Katie's wide eyes looked at Wasyl again. "It's true," he mouthed. Katie slid closer to her sisters and didn't look at Wasyl again.

* * *

That night in bed, Katie tossed and turned. She squeezed her eyes shut and tried to sleep again, but it was no use. The house was completely dark, and the only sounds were those of Mama, Wasyl, and her sisters softly breathing in their sleep. Finally, she couldn't stand it any longer. She nudged Tillie, who was sound asleep next to her. No response. She nudged her again. Tillie groaned a little and moved over. Well, Katie decided, Tillie wasn't going to be any help at all. She reached over Tillie and tapped Mary on the back. Mary stirred. Desperately, Katie shook Mary's shoulder.

"Huh?" mumbled Mary, turning over.

"I need to visit the outhouse," whispered Katie.

"Well, go ahead," replied Mary. "I don't."

"I'm scared," Katie persisted.

"Take Prince with you," Mary whispered, and then turned her back as though the matter were settled.

Katie looked around the dark room, biting her lip. She had no choice. Prince was a big dog, she reasoned. Prince would protect her. She slid off the bed, and her feet landed on the cold, bare floor. "Here, Prince. Here, boy," she whispered as she made her way to the door. Prince slowly stretched and looked up at Katie. "Come on, boy. Outside!" Katie commanded.

Prince really didn't look too eager to leave his warm spot by the stove, but he obeyed anyway. Stepping out on the back porch, Katie quickly surveyed the yard. Prince sniffed around the ground. The not quite full moon cast shadows over the sparse grass and the apple tree. That looming black shape to the right was Mama's grape arbor, Katie reminded herself. At the end of the path, sheltered by the peach tree near the fence, sat the small, whitewashed outhouse.

She started across the yard, looking this way and that so that "something" would not get her. She was almost there. Katie shivered and looked over her shoulder. What was it that Wasyl had said earlier about a ghost passing by? Suddenly, she heard the haunting wail of a stray tomcat and the answering moan from another. Where was Prince? Her heart beating fast, she ran the remaining steps to the outhouse, bounded inside, slammed the door, and slid the lock in place.

What a relief! She sat down and waited for her heart to stop pounding. Soon she was ready to return to the house. Suddenly, she heard Prince barking in the yard. What was there? Did he see the ghost that had made her shiver? Prince was barking nonstop right outside the outhouse door now. Oh, no! The ghost must be out there waiting for her!

Katie shivered again. That meant another ghost must be in here with her!

"Mama!" Katie screamed. "Mama! Mama!"

Prince was barking wildly now and jumping at the outhouse door. His barking became fainter and then louder as Katie huddled in a corner of the outhouse and continued to scream, "Mama!"

"Katie! Katie!" called a familiar voice from outside. "Katie, unlock this door. It's Mama."

Sobbing, Katie unlocked the door and tumbled into Mama's arms. Prince circled them, wagging his tail and licking them wherever he could. Mama put her arm around Katie's trembling shoulders and led her back to the house.

Once inside, Mama took Katie on her lap. They sat in the old wooden rocking chair by the stove, and Mama threw her warm shawl over them both. When Katie had calmed down and stopped shivering, she told Mama about feeling the ghosts pass by, one in the yard and one inside the outhouse.

Mama sighed. "Oh, Katie, ghost stories are just that—only stories. People tell them because they think it is fun to scare others, not because they are true. I have heard ghost stories all my life, repeated over and over, each time changed a little bit to suit the storyteller or his listeners. That doesn't make those stories true, but I will tell you something that is true. In my entire life, I have never seen a ghost. I think I would have if they were real. Don't you? And as for shivering—well, it doesn't take a ghost to make you shiver on a chilly night like this."

Mama chuckled, and Katie relaxed. She snuggled close to Mama. As they rocked, Mama stroked Katie's hair and softly sang one of the old minor key songs she had learned from her own Mama long ago in Old Country. Katie awoke in the morning in her own cozy place in the big bed.

## Chapter 5

Adeline was true to her word. Katie let her help peel potatoes after school, and on Saturdays, Adeline treated Katie to the picture shows at the Nickelette. Even though they couldn't read well enough to know everything the actors were saying, they thought the slapstick comedies were hilarious. Sometimes they made up their own dialogue and laughed even harder. If Adeline's father gave her an extra nickel, they stopped for a bag of hot roasted peanuts to share on the way home.

However, this Saturday, Mama told her children that they were all going to pick coal. Katie wanted to invite Adeline to come along, but Mama said, "No, there will be no time for play today, and Adeline's mother probably doesn't want her getting all dirty picking coal anyway." So, Katie had to tell her friend that this Saturday was a workday for the family, as all the following Saturdays and some afternoons after school would be, until they had a good supply of coal stored for the long winter ahead.

The autumn air was crisp, and the sun was bright in the sky when they started out Saturday morning. Mama pushed the wooden wheelbarrow piled with burlap sacks and buckets behind the small frame houses of their

Ukrainian, Polish, and Slovak neighborhood. They headed toward the gritty outskirts of Plymouth, where the culm banks sat near the mines. As they approached the huge mountains of waste coal and slate that dotted the anthracite region, Katie could see dozens of other women and children already busy gleaning coal.

Katie, Tillie, Mary, and Wasyl each took a bucket and spread out on the steep slope of the refuse pile. They started searching for the occasional nuggets of good coal that had been discarded. When they had a full bucket, they took it to the wheelbarrow and emptied their heavy load into one of the burlap sacks. Mama picked coal directly into the old apron she wore because there weren't enough buckets for everyone to use.

It was a long afternoon of tedious searching through the culm. When a likely lump was picked up, they examined it to determine the quality. If Katie wasn't sure, she would ask Mary or Mama if it was good or not. Mama's goal was ten buckets of coal that day, and Katie knew that she must not cheat on either the quality or the quantity, or her family would be very cold that winter. Even Wasyl wasn't tempted to put any rocks in the bottom of his bucket just to make it fill up faster.

Finally, the last of the coal was loaded onto the wheelbarrow. Three big burlap sacks had been filled and tied closed with a piece of frayed rope. Mama rubbed her back and sighed. "Ahh," she said, "more than ten buckets. It has been a good day." Mama smiled a tired smile.

Katie was so tired from trudging up and down the culm bank searching for coal to fill her bucket, which grew heavier with each added chunk of coal, but she was happy that she had helped to make Mama smile. It made Katie feel good inside to be helping, important, and needed—almost grown-up. Someday, when she had a job, she thought, then she really would help Mama.

Slowly, the weary family headed for home, the heavy sacks of coal jostling in the wheelbarrow Mama pushed over the bumpy ground. They could hear an approaching train as their little procession neared the railroad tracks. Wo-o-o, wo-o-o! it whistled in warning. The children waved vigorously at the engineer, and he smiled in return and threw a handful of hard candy in their direction. Katie scrambled to grab two lemon drops. Mama surveyed the scene to be sure that each child had a piece of candy.

"Katie got two!" Wasyl complained.

"But she's going to share one with Mama," Mary immediately answered. "Isn't that right, Katie?"

Silently, Katie held up a piece of candy to Mama.

"Thank you, my little one. The Lord will reward your kindness," praised Mama, and they savored the sweet treats and continued on the dusty path toward home.

*** 

After a supper of warm cabbage soup and thick slices of homemade bread, they hauled a large, galvanized tub out onto the floor near the coal stove. Mama started heating big kettles of water on the stove while the girls cleaned off the table, did the dishes, and swept the kitchen floor. Wasyl fed Prince and gave him fresh water, then he carried the bowl of kitchen scraps outside to bury them in the garden before it got dark.

Mama filled the big tub partway with cold water from the sink, then she added a kettle of boiling water. Every Saturday, they took turns being first. Today it was Katie's turn to have the first bath. Because she was first, the water was not very deep, but it was all clean. While Mama scrubbed Katie, Tillie and Mary took turns washing their hair with yellow soap in the white enamel basin in the sink.

After Katie was done with her bath, Mama added another kettle full of boiling water for Mary's turn in the tub. Then, Mama led Katie to the sink where she attacked Katie's hair with vigor, scrubbing with yellow soap until Katie's scalp tingled. When she was done rinsing Katie's hair with cold vinegar water, Mama added another pot of boiling water to the tub for Tillie's bath and then turned to Wasyl. He hated to have his hair washed and always howled throughout the entire process, but Mama showed no mercy when it came to Saturday night baths and head scrubbing. Finally, another pot of boiling water, and Wasyl was the last one in the tub.

Content that her children were all scrubbed pink and tucked in for the night, Mama took a large bucket and started to empty the bathwater from the tub. She carried each bucketful of dirty water out to the garden and individually watered her tomato, zucchini, and cucumber plants until the roots were well soaked. This not only gave the plants a good drink, but the soapy water also worked as an insecticide to keep bugs away from her precious garden.

Katie's eyelids were growing heavy as she listened to Mama bustle in and around as quietly as she could. She knew that after the children and the garden were taken care of, Mama would refill the tub for herself. After Mama's bath, the big, galvanized tub would again be emptied, wiped dry, and stored away until next Saturday night.

## Chapter 6

Sunday was Katie's favorite day. It was so special—like a holiday. On Sundays, Mama didn't have to go to work on The Flats or cook dinner for the boarders. Mama said that Sunday was a day of rest for everyone. The children didn't have school, and best of all, Ann came home from the Weises, where she lived and worked all week as a housekeeper.

Ann was fourteen years old. She was taller than Mama, and she wore her glossy dark hair in two long braids. Katie thought that Ann seemed so grown up, almost like a lady now that she had a full-time job and lived uptown. Ann always came home on Sunday mornings because that was her day off. She shared Mama's bed on Sunday night and left for work again early Monday morning. The family wouldn't see her again until the following Sunday.

A tap, tap, tap on the door announced her arrival. Before anyone could move, she threw open the door and announced, "Hello, everybody! I'm home!"

Prince yipped and wiggled all over, licking her rough red fingers. Mama drew her rosy-cheeked oldest daughter inside with a hug, a steaming cup of coffee, and warm buttered toast. The children finished their breakfast and gave Ann all the news about school and the neighborhood. In turn, Ann talked about her duties and activities at the Weises.

The discussion continued, but more subdued, as the family walked the two blocks to St. Vladimir's Ukrainian Church. Upon entering the church, Katie knew better than to talk. She sat through the service in wide-eyed wonder. Everything was so grand and majestic in the church. The golden gates of the sanctuary glowed in the candlelight. Incense wafted on the air. The priest's regal robes swished around the altar as he paraded the Holy Scriptures before the worshippers. The priest was charged with explaining the mysteries of the Bible because most of his congregation couldn't read it for themselves.

Katie glanced around at the devout parishioners and noticed some familiar faces from her neighborhood. The immigrants sat enthralled, drinking in the sounds of the church service being conducted in their native language. Katie looked up at Mama during the singing. Mama sang with all her heart, enjoying the ancient hymns she had learned long ago in a distant land. Mama had once told the children that when she sang, she was remembering loved ones who were still in Old Country, worshipping in a church very much like this one and singing the same hymns that she now sang in America. Sometimes, Katie thought she saw tears in Mama's eyes as she sang.

After church, the family leisurely strolled along Main Street toward home.

"Mama, Pearl and her sister invited me to go hiking in the hills this afternoon," Ann said. "We want to take a picnic dinner along. May I go with them?"

Mama smiled and nodded her approval. Ann worked hard all week, and Mama was glad to see her have some fun with other girls her age on a Sunday.

"It's just as well," Mama said. "Titka Catherine will be coming to visit this afternoon."

Everyone fell quiet as they neared the house.

"Why?" Mary finally asked.

"She says that it has been a long time since she came to visit," Mama replied. "And I told her that she is always welcome…and we will welcome her." Mama gave them all a stern look.

"Honestly, Mama, I don't know how you can be so nice to her. I'm glad I won't be there," Ann said. "She never has anything good to say about anyone, and…"

"Enough!" Mama snapped. "It doesn't cost anything to be polite. Understand?"

She looked at each child in turn until they answered, "Yes, Mama."

When they got home, Ann packed her lunch and left for Pearl's house as quickly as she could.

The other children and Mama stayed in their good clothes because company was coming. In honor of Sunday, lunch was simply cold sandwiches and water with little fuss. Mama was strict about keeping the Lord's Day holy, and cooking was work. The older girls knew better than to embroider or crochet on Sundays, and Katie was not allowed to use Mama's scissors to cut out paper dolls.

Mama said that cutting on Sunday was a sin. Anyone who even tried to snip a stray thread from their clothing on a Sunday invoked Mama's wrath, which, if it were any indication of God's feelings on the matter, should be avoided at all costs.

Just as the older girls were clearing off the table, Katie, who had been drawing pictures on the misty windowpane, announced, "Here comes Titka Catherine."

Mary and Tillie rushed to the window. "Oh no," said Mary. "She's brought Julia and Nellie with her."

"Ugh." Tillie groaned.

"Wasyl, hold Prince," Mama commanded. "Now, girls…" She gave them all a meaningful look before she patted her tidy, fair bun and threw open the door.

"Catherine, welcome," Mama said as her older sister flounced in followed by two miniature versions of her haughty self, twelve-year-old Julia and ten-year old Nellie.

Wasyl dragged the growling dog past their visitors and chained him outside under the apple tree. He used this opportunity to stay outside.

Because it was Sunday, the girls had to visit quietly among themselves. They sat on the bed while Mama and Titka drank their coffee and chatted at the table. Katie watched Tillie and Nellie play tic-tac-toe on Tillie's slate.

"I see you are using the kitchen rugs I gave you," Katie heard Titka Catherine remark as her plump fingers indicated the clean, but obviously worn, carpets strategically placed over the high traffic areas on Mama's immaculate floor.

"Yes," Mama replied. "Rag rugs do help to keep the floor warm."

"We got new rugs," Julia said to Mary, her auburn curls bobbing up and down as she spoke.

"So?" Mary responded, not looking up as they played Cat's Cradle with a long circle of string.

"I brought this bag of clothes," Titka continued, handing a large brown paper bag to Mama. "They should fit one of your girls. Julia and Nellie are growing so fast that I even had to buy them new shoes. You'll find their old shoes in the bottom of the bag. I think there is still some wear in them. If they don't fit Mary or Tillie, then Katie will grow into them sooner or later."

Mary and Tillie paused and eyed the bag suspiciously from across the room. Katie knew that her sisters hated to wear Nellie's and Julia's hand-me-downs because their cousins had the habit of reminding them loudly, so that everyone around was sure to hear, "That used to be my dress," or, "Those are my old shoes." Katie always wore her sisters' outgrown clothing and didn't mind much at all, but she understood how Mary and Tillie felt. Hand-me-downs from Julia and Nellie were not a blessing to enjoy but a burden to bear.

"Where is Ann? I thought she was home today," said Titka Catherine, glancing around. "Such a pity you only get to see her on Sundays."

"She is hiking with her girlfriends," Mama replied. "They will stop in the country for a picnic before returning home."

"Humph! I don't know why you allow her to wander over the countryside unescorted. How unbecoming for a young lady!" clucked Titka Catherine.

"She's not alone," said Mama.

"It's bad enough that she lives away from home all week. Who knows what she's doing while she's away?"

"I know what she's doing," Mama said firmly. "She's being a good girl and working hard. Every Sunday, she hands me her pay, which helps to put food on our table. I trust her."

"Mark my words," warned Titka Catherine, shaking her finger in an ominous way. "Any fourteen-year-old girl who has that much freedom will come to no good!" She turned to Mary, Tillie, and Katie and said pointedly, "Now, if you girls ever want to know what to do or how to behave properly, just look at my girls. Nellie and Julia are excellent examples for you to follow." Nellie and Julia tilted their chins a little higher and smiled smugly.

"Ann is a good girl," Mama slowly repeated between clenched teeth.

Katie, eager to escape the inevitable clash, asked, "Mama, may we go out in the yard? We won't get dirty," she promised.

"Yes, you may all go outside," Mama said.

Titka Catherine nodded her permission to her daughters. The girls seized this opportunity to join Wasyl and Prince in the warm autumn sunshine.

Prince had found a spot of sun and was basking his glossy black coat in its warmth. Wasyl had three apples, which he was using to practice juggling. It was such a peaceful scene. Prince, reclining in the sun, watched the shiny red apples go up in the air, down, then up again as one by one, Wasyl threw them up and caught them in rhythm.

"You're getting good!" said Tillie.

"Really good!" Julia agreed.

Wasyl blushed. "Here, want one?" He offered two of the apples he had been juggling to his cousins.

"Ugh! No!" said Nellie, stepping in front of Julia. "You touched it. We'll just pick a clean apple from the tree." She reached up for a tempting red apple.

"No, don't!" yelled Wasyl, but Nellie ignored him and plucked the apple just as a black flash sprang into the air.

With his powerful front paws on her shoulders, Prince knocked Nellie onto the ground. She landed on her back with the dog standing over her, growling menacingly. Nellie's wide eyes stared at Prince in terror. Julia screamed. Katie was speechless.

"Drop the apple! Drop the apple!" Tillie and Mary yelled.

Nellie opened her hand, and the apple rolled to the ground. Prince started panting and wagging his tail.

"Good dog!" Wasyl said. "Good boy!" He ruffled the dog's furry head and patted his back. "Good boy!"

Nellie got to her feet and dusted herself off. She wasn't really hurt, but it was obvious her pride was injured. "Good dog?" She scoffed. "How can you say that? He attacked me!"

"You shouldn't take things that don't belong to you," Mary countered.

"We trained Prince, and he's a good watchdog," Wasyl said. "If you had just asked, then we would have picked an apple for you. That would be all right. But never ever try to take anything from this property yourself, or Prince will stop you."

"Humph!" said Julia indignantly. "You don't have anything we'd want anyway, and I'm telling!" She flounced across the yard. As she entered the kitchen, loud voices filtered through the open door, then it slammed shut again.

Katie was afraid that Mama would punish them for allowing Prince to attack Nellie, but in a moment, Titka Catherine and Julia hustled out of the house, collecting Nellie on their way out of the yard. The look on Mama's face showed that she was grateful for their guests' hasty departure.

Trying to be polite, Katie called out after her aunt and cousins, "Please come again soon!"

"Humph!" snorted Julia, her nose in the air, as she marched behind her mother and younger sister.

## Chapter 7

Katie stood at the basin washing her face and hands before breakfast. Glancing out the frosty window to her right, she could see some neighborhood children getting water from the alley pump. They must be so cold out there this morning, she thought. The five other families on their street shared the pump because their houses had no indoor plumbing. At least we have a cold-water pipe in the kitchen. How I would hate to carry all our water from the outside pump.

As she watched, she noticed a snowflake fall, then two, then three. "It's snowing! It's snowing!" she shouted. Her brother and sisters came to the window to see.

"I hope we get lots and lots of snow," said Wasyl. "Then we can have snowball fights."

"Oh, Mama," moaned Mary, "Frankie Leskovich is out at the pump in his bare feet again."

"Go, shoo him home," said Mama. "With a new baby to care for, his mama probably didn't even see how he was dressed when he ran outside. The **grippe** is going around, and he'll get it next if he gets chilled."

Mary pulled on her coat and hurried outside. Katie

watched through the window as Mary grabbed little Frankie's thin hand. She shook her finger in his face as she scolded the startled youngster, then with a quick swat to his bottom, she sent him scurrying back to his own door. Poor Frankie, thought Katie. Tomorrow he'll probably be out at the pump in his bare feet again. He never seems to learn.

"Mama, what's wrong with Frankie? He always gets into trouble. He never learns. Why doesn't he ever behave?"

Mama sighed. "Katie, some people are not as fortunate as we are. Some people do not come into this world with a strong, healthy body. Some others do not have a strong, healthy mind. That is how it is with Frankie. He will always need others to care for him and protect him. He was only two years old when the twins were born, and now his mama has the new baby to care for, too. She just can't watch Frankie all the time. That's why everyone must help her to watch over him—so he will be safe. Do you understand?"

"Yes, Mama," Katie replied.

Mary swept through the doorway in a blast of frigid air. "Brr-r-r," she said, hurrying to the stove. "It's really starting to come down now. We'll have snow for Thanksgiving for sure."

"Yippee!" squealed Wasyl, dancing a joyful little jig.

A new thought struck Katie. "Mama, will Ann get to come home for Thanksgiving?"

"Oh, dear, no," Mama answered. "The Weises will have a big dinner and lots of company. They will need Ann then more than ever. We will see her on Sunday, as usual."

Katie looked down and sighed. Her shoulders drooped.

"Oh, cheer up, Katie," said Tillie.

"Yeah, cheer up," said Wasyl. "Mama is going to make a big roast chicken dinner for us on Thursday, and I get to help butcher Ella!"

"What?" demanded Katie. Ella was Mama's biggest hen. Katie saw her every day and talked to her when she fed the chickens. Ella was almost a pet. "We're eating Ella for Thanksgiving? Why can't we eat turkey on Thanksgiving?"

"Because we have chickens, and chicken we will eat!" said Mama.

Katie knew that Mama was a woman of her word. If she said they were eating Ella on Thanksgiving, then that was exactly what they would do. Katie was not looking forward to Thursday. She tossed and turned all night worrying about poor Ella. How could Katie watch her family eat her pet? It would be impossible. What could she do?

\* \* \*

The next day at school, Katie explained her problem to Adeline.

"Well, just come to my house for Thanksgiving," said Adeline. "My aunt Gertrude is coming from New York. You'll like her. My mother won't mind if I tell her that we will peel the potatoes. Okay?"

Katie liked that idea, so that evening, she brought up the subject. "Mama, Adeline invited me to have Thanksgiving dinner at her house. Please, may I go? Please? I can't be thankful if I see Ella all roasted up on the table. Please don't make me." Katie's eyes filled with tears, and she continued, "They are having company, and Adeline told her mother that we would peel the potatoes…and I can help with other things, too." Katie looked hopefully up at her mother.

Mama thought for a moment, then she smiled. "Well, if they really need your help, and since Adeline has helped you peel potatoes so many times, then I think it will be all right for you to help her on Thanksgiving."

Katie smiled. "Adeline said they will eat dinner at noon, so I should leave early on Thursday so I can help all morning." Then I won't be around when Ella is butchered, thought Katie.

"That sounds like a good idea," Mama agreed.

Wasyl rolled his eyes. "Girls!" he muttered.

Katie said goodbye to Ella as she fed the chickens after school the next day. She would never talk to her again, but Ella didn't know that, so Katie tried to sound cheerful as Ella clucked and pecked at the ground around Katie's feet. Poor Ella.

## Chapter 8

Thanksgiving Day finally arrived. Katie was so excited! Not only did she not have to eat Ella, but there was no school, and she was allowed to spend the entire day with her best friend.

Katie was up before Mama even started making breakfast. She tried to be extra quiet as she filled the basin with cold water and washed her face and hands so she wouldn't wake her brother and sisters.

"Mama," whispered Katie, "may I wear my Sunday dress?"

"No," said Mama. "Save that dress for Sunday. I have a surprise for you."

She pulled a box from under her bed and lifted out a dress that Katie recognized from the bag of clothes that Titka Catherine had brought. It was dark blue with a white collar and white buttons down the back.

"For me?" Katie asked, her eyes widening with delight.

"Yes, Little One. I had to alter it a bit and take up the hem, but I think this will be perfect for today."

"Oh, Mama, thank you!" Katie wrapped her arms

around Mama's waist. She ate a quick breakfast of hot oatmeal, buttered toast, and creamy coffee. She slipped into the new-to-her dress, then Mama helped her with the buttons and ran a comb through Katie's short hair. The entire process of bundling up for the cold weather—boots, coat, **babushka**, and mittens—seemed to take forever, but at last, she was ready. She gave Mama a quick kiss goodbye just as Wasyl was waking up, then she was on her way uptown.

Because it was so cold, or maybe because she was so excited, the walk to Adeline's seemed longer than she remembered. Main Street was empty since it was a holiday morning. She covered her nose and cheeks with her mittened hands when they started to sting from the frigid air, but she kept walking briskly toward her friend's house.

By the time she reached the tavern, her cheeks and nose were red, and her fingers and toes were cold and tingly. She trudged up the back steps and knocked on the door. Adeline answered and pulled Katie into the warm kitchen already filled with the aroma of turkey roasting in the coal oven. "I'm so glad you're here!" said Adeline.

"Me, too," said Katie pulling off her boots and untying her babushka. She was rubbing her hands together by the stove just as Mrs. Adams and her sister entered the room.

"Hello, Katie," said Mrs. Adams.

"Hello, Mrs. Adams," said Katie. Remembering her manners, she added, "Thank you for inviting me for Thanksgiving."

"Well, I never refuse help in the kitchen." Mrs. Adams winked.

"Aunt Gertrude," interrupted Adeline, "this is my friend, Katie. She's in my class at school."

"It's a pleasure to finally meet the famous Katie I've heard so much about. I hear you two are expert potato peelers," said Adeline's aunt.

Katie and Adeline giggled. "Katie taught me how," said Adeline. "We are pretty good."

With that, Mrs. Adams plunked a sack of potatoes on the table and two potato peelers. "That's all?" asked Katie, and the girls giggled again. They explained that when Adeline helped peel potatoes at Katie's house after school, they usually peeled twice as many. Katie's family and the boarders ate a lot of potatoes.

While Adeline and Katie worked on the potatoes, they talked about school and quizzed each other on the spelling words Miss Wint had assigned that week. Meanwhile, Mrs. Adams prepared the rest of the meal, and Aunt Gertrude was busy in the dining room setting the table for their feast.

"All finished!" said Adeline and Katie.

"Fine," said Mrs. Adams. "Please clean off the table now. Scoop all the peelings into that bucket underneath, and then wipe off the table and dry it well. Then you may play in Adeline's room. We'll call you when it's time to eat. Thank you for helping, girls."

In Adeline's room, there was plenty to do. She had checkers, a card game, and several dolls. Katie drifted toward the doll on Adeline's bed. She was so pretty! She had long dark hair and eyes that opened and closed. The girls didn't notice Aunt Gertrude standing in the doorway.

"Go on," said Adeline. "You may play with her. Her name is Sophie."

Katie carefully lifted Sophie from the bed. "Ma-ma," cried Sophie.

"Oh!" Katie gasped in wonder. "She talks! I didn't know dolls could talk."

"Well, she can only say 'Ma-ma,' and only when she sits up. She doesn't know any other words," said Adeline.

Aunt Gertrude chuckled in the doorway. "Don't your dolls talk, Katie?" asked Aunt Gertrude.

"I don't have any dolls," said Katie, making Sophie say Ma-ma again.

"But Katie has three sisters and a brother, so she always has real people to play with," said Adeline.

"Really?" said Aunt Gertrude. "Tell me about your family."

"Well, Ann is the oldest. She's fourteen, but she doesn't live with us because she keeps house for the Weises all week. She comes home on Sundays. Then there's Mary. She's eleven. Tillie is nine. Wasyl just turned eight, and then there's me," said Katie. "We also have a dog. His name is Prince."

"You do have plenty of playmates," said Aunt Gertrude. "And your mother and father?"

"My father was a miner, but he died when I was a baby. I don't even remember him. Mama takes care of us and the boarders, and she works on The Flats when I'm in school."

"Your Mama sounds like a busy woman," said Aunt Gertrude.

"I guess she is," said Katie, still cradling Sophie and gazing at her pretty face.

Just then, a little bell tinkled, and Aunt Gertrude said that meant dinner was ready. Katie gently returned Sophie to the bed and followed Adeline and Aunt Gertrude to the dining room.

Mr. Adams was already seated at the head of the table but rose when they entered. "That's some fancy dinner bell you brought us, Gertrude," he said.

"Oh, it's just a little gift from my store. I had to contribute something to the meal, and food doesn't travel very well," replied Aunt Gertrude. "I'm glad you like it."

Katie surveyed the feast on the table. It all looked and smelled so delicious, but what she really noticed were the lace tablecloth and gleaming crystal glassware. A lace tablecloth!

When everyone was seated, Mr. Adams cleared his throat and said, "Now, we will say grace." Everyone bowed their heads as Mr. Adams thanked God for another good year. He asked Him to bless their food and grant God's favor on everyone at the table. He also prayed for protection for the brave American soldiers on foreign soil. At the end, everyone chimed in, "Amen!"

Katie had never seen so much food at one time. She especially liked the stuffing and cranberry sauce. Mr. Adams joked that the mashed potatoes came out perfectly because they had been peeled by "experts." He complimented Mrs. Adams on the fine turkey, roasted to perfection, and she smiled.

Katie only had a tiny piece of turkey, because seeing that huge roasted bird reminded her of Ella, poor Ella, who was at that very moment being served on her own family's Thanksgiving table. She shook the thought from her mind.

Just when Katie thought she couldn't hold another bite of food, Mrs. Adams said, "I hope everyone saved room for dessert."

"What's dessert?" Katie whispered to Adeline as they helped clear the table.

"Oh, you'll like it. Mother has been baking for days. We have apple pie, pumpkin pie, and mincemeat pie. If you don't like pie, then we also have cinnamon coffeecake," said Adeline, rubbing her stomach and licking her lips.

Katie tried a sliver of pumpkin pie and a small piece of apple pie. She liked them both, but thought the pumpkin pie was the best. She never knew you could put apples in a pie. She wondered why Mama never made pies from the apples that grew on their tree. The mincemeat pie didn't look very appealing to Katie, so she didn't taste any of that. When Mrs. Adams offered her a piece of cinnamon coffeecake, Katie wanted to try that also, but she said, "No, thank you," because she was stuffed.

The girls offered to help dry the dishes, but Aunt Gertrude took that job so they could return to Adeline's room and play until it was time for Katie to leave. They decided to play checkers, but pretended the dolls were playing. Adeline said that Katie could be Sophie while Adeline would be Johnny, a smaller baby doll. Taking turns, each girl made her doll push the checkers across the board. Sophie won one game, crying, "Ma-ma!" with each move, and Johnny won two. "He plays very well for a baby!" said Katie. Aunt Gertrude came in just as they were giggling about that comment.

"Okay, Adeline, let's walk Katie home before it starts getting dark," said Aunt Gertrude.

The girls jumped up and started to pick up the checkers game. Katie tenderly placed Sophie back on the bed after making her say, "Ma-ma!" one more time. As they left the room, she turned and softly said, "Goodbye, Sophie."

In the kitchen, Mrs. Adams handed a paper-wrapped parcel to Aunt Gertrude. "Please give this to Katie's mother. I noticed that Katie didn't get to taste my cinnamon coffeecake, so I'm sending enough for her to share with her family."

"Oh, thank you!" said Katie. She couldn't wait to tell her brother and sisters all about dessert.

* * *

It was a little warmer now than when Katie had walked to Adeline's that morning, and the walk was so much more fun with Adeline and Aunt Gertrude strolling along. Aunt Gertrude described bustling New York City, where she lived. She told them about her job in a big department store, but she said she would only work there until she got married next summer.

"Married! You're getting married?" said Adeline, suddenly stopping.

"Why, yes," said Aunt Gertrude. "Next year, you will have an Uncle Alfred. He works in another big store in the city."

"That's so exciting!" said Adeline. "I've never had an uncle before. Will I like him? Is he nice?"

Aunt Gertrude blushed. "Oh, yes," she said. "He's very nice."

Soon they turned off Main Street, and Katie led them down the narrow alley that ended in her neighborhood by the railroad tracks.

"This is where you live?" asked Aunt Gertrude as she surveyed the coal-dusted immigrant shanties and rickety fences. The rutted dirt road was not more than a path, slippery with scattered mounds of frozen slush, so they stepped very carefully.

"My house is just past the pump," said Katie.

She led them up to the back stoop and held the door open for Aunt Gertrude and Adeline to enter the warm kitchen. They all stood on the long rag rug by the door so their soggy boots wouldn't dirty Mama's scrubbed wooden floor. Katie began to remove her boots, so they did the same.

Mama turned from the stove. "Mama," said Katie, "Adeline and her aunt Gertrude walked me home."

Prince immediately jumped up to sniff the visitors. "Hello, Prince," said Aunt Gertrude, offering the back of her hand for him to sniff. At the sound of his name, Prince wagged his tail in greeting.

"Oh, come in, come in," urged Mama. "I have hot coffee to warm you up while your boots dry." She gathered their boots and placed them near the stove. Then she pulled out some chairs at the table and motioned for them to come over. "Sit, sit," she said.

Tillie and Mary hustled to get cups and spoons for the visitors, while Mama placed sugar and cream on the table. Mama added extra hot water and cream to Adeline and Katie's cups of coffee, so it was sweet and only mildly coffee flavored, but Aunt Gertrude said she liked her coffee black. The hot cups of coffee warmed their cold fingers as they sipped and visited.

Aunt Gertrude told Mama that Katie and Adeline were both great helpers today, peeling potatoes and clearing the table after dinner. Mama seemed pleased to hear that. Katie told Mama about Sophie, the doll who could say "Ma-ma." Adeline said that Aunt Gertrude was getting married next summer. Aunt Gertrude blushed again.

"That is nice." Mama clasped her hands together and said, "I wish you and your young man a happy life together. God bless you!"

"Thank you," said Aunt Gertrude. "Oh, I almost forgot." She slid the package across the table toward Mama. "It's some of the dessert Katie didn't get to try, so my sister sent enough for your whole family to have some. I hope you like it."

"Dessert?" Mama looked confused.

"You will love it, Mama," Katie said, rubbing her stomach. Adeline nodded her head and licked her lips in the direction of Tillie and Mary.

"Thank you," said Mama as she accepted the package.

"And thank you for the coffee," said Aunt Gertrude, smiling. "Now we must be on our way, or it will be dark before we reach home."

Mama retrieved their now dry and toasty boots so they could start out again. "Thank you for walking me home," said Katie as she waved goodbye and closed the door behind them.

Mama looked at Katie. "What is dessert?" she asked as she held up the package.

"That's cinnamon coffeecake, but dessert can be anything sweet you eat after dinner," explained Katie. "Today I also had pumpkin pie and apple pie. Mama, did you know you could make pies with apples? We have an apple tree, so we should do that."

"Maybe someday you will," said Mama with a twinkle in her eye. "I don't have time for that, too."

That night after a simple dinner of Thanksgiving leftovers, all the children and Mama each had a piece of Mrs. Adams's cinnamon coffeecake. Everyone agreed that dessert is delicious.

# Chapter 9

All the crops had been harvested. The fields on The Flats had been plowed under to wait for the next spring thaw so planting could begin again. Northeastern Pennsylvania was in the grip of winter's harshest weather, so there was no work on the farms for Mama and the other immigrant laborers. They still earned income from the boarders, but money was even scarcer than usual. Katie didn't really understand, but sometimes she saw Mama stop in the middle of her household chores, bow her head, and whisper a prayer. She knew Mama was worried.

One good thing about Mama not going out to work every day, though, was that she could attend the Christmas Program at school. All the parents were invited to come the afternoon of the last day of school before winter vacation began. Each class would perform something special. Katie's and Wasyl's class of first and second graders had been practicing a Christmas song. Tillie and Mary would each say a "**piece**" they had been assigned to memorize. Only the best students in the upper elementary grades had been selected to say a piece, so it was quite an honor to be chosen. They practiced at home every evening so they wouldn't make any mistakes.

Katie wanted Mama to see her classroom, and she couldn't wait to give her the Christmas card she had made. Mama said that she had never gone to school when she was a child, and that her children should be very grateful to have that opportunity. She explained that in **Old Country**, only boys went to school, and then just until they learned to read, write, and do basic math. The boys just needed enough education to be able to run a farm. Only the wealthy boys attended school after that. Girls in Old Country didn't go to school at all. They stayed at home and learned from their mothers how to take care of the house, sew, cook, garden, and care for babies.

The parents of the students in Katie's school were also asked to donate cookies or a baked treat to share after the Christmas Program, so it would be like a party. Mama said that she would make **chrusciki** for the special occasion. Katie was so excited!

"Mama," asked Katie one evening, "will Santa Clause come to our house on Christmas Eve? I wish he would bring me a doll."

Mama's brow furrowed. She pressed her lips together, but she didn't answer. Katie waited and then asked again, "Mama, do you think he will bring me a doll? ... Mama?"

"Katie," said Mary. "Stop pestering. Dolls are for rich people. You have to pay Santa, you know. He doesn't just give presents away. He might not come here at all."

"Oh," said Katie.

Wasyl and Tillie glanced at each other but didn't say a word. Mama continued mending holes in the girls' long, black stockings, which were more mend than stocking by now. She didn't say a word either.

*　*　*

The next day at school, Adeline and Katie talked about Christmas. "I don't think I will hang my stocking this year," said Katie. "Mary said you have to pay Santa, so he only comes to your house if you are rich."

"That's not true," said Adeline. "He comes to our house, and we're not rich."

"I think you're richer than we are," said Katie.

She tried not to think about Santa or stockings or what might be in them on Christmas morning. Instead, she tried to concentrate on the Christmas Program; it was only one week away. Katie loved practicing "Away in a Manger," the song her class would sing for their parents. It comforted her to think about baby Jesus, snuggled in the hay and surrounded by gentle animals and adoring Mary and Joseph.

Although her class knew the words to all three verses of their song, they still practiced every day. Miss Wint reminded them to project their voices and to enunciate clearly. "Remember, boys and girls, if people can't hear or understand the words, then your song loses its meaning."

Finally, the big day arrived! When the children came home for lunch the day of the Christmas Program, Mama had a big pan of chrusciki ready to go. Such a rare treat!

They all looked forward to tasting the flaky angel-wing pastries, heavily dusted with powdered sugar. Mama covered the pan with a clean white cloth and allowed Mary to carry it all the way to school.

When they arrived, Mary headed straight to the auditorium to drop off their contribution to the Christmas celebration. Following behind, Mama paused to peep into the younger children's classrooms as Katie, Wasyl, and Tillie pointed to where their desks were located. The teachers were bustling to organize all the excited students, so Mama proceeded to join the other parents waiting in the auditorium. On either side of the large room, long tables were set up to hold the donated treats and pitchers of iced tea. A Christmas tree, decorated with red and green paper chains and ornaments the children had made, stood at the front. It all looked very festive.

Soon it was time for Katie's class to file to the front. She searched the audience as she took her place among her classmates. There was Mama's smiling face! Katie smiled back and chanced a tiny wave. She sang "Away in a Manger" with all her heart. Some of the parents joined in, and everyone clapped at the end. Katie beamed and thought, That was easy.

She was glad she didn't have to stand alone in front of this crowd and say a piece like her sisters. Just the thought made Katie shiver, but Tillie and Mary had practiced until they both knew their pieces by heart. Her sisters said their pieces perfectly, and Tillie even remembered to add a little curtsy at the end.

Afterward, Adeline's mother drifted over to Mama and wished her a Merry Christmas. Mama smiled and responded in Ukrainian. Katie offered Adeline and Mrs. Adams some chrusciki and explained that Russian children called them angel wings because of how they were shaped.

Adeline grabbed Katie's hands and said, "Guess what! Aunt Gertrude is coming to visit us the day after Christmas!"

"Why the day after?" asked Katie. "Doesn't she want to celebrate Christmas with you?"

"Oh, she would love to," cut in Mrs. Adams, "but her store will be very busy with holiday shoppers right up until Christmas day. So, she will come the day after and spend a few days with us. Gertrude hopes that Katie will be allowed to come over and visit while she is in town." She glanced at Mama, then Katie.

"Please, may I? Please, Mama?" Katie asked.

"I suppose I could spare Katie for one day during Christmas vacation," said Mama, so the mothers agreed on December 28. Katie and Adeline clapped their hands and hugged.

## Chapter 10

The twenty-fourth day of December dawned cold and gray with large, fluffy snowflakes tumbling from the sky. The day before, sensing a storm brewing, Mama and the children had picked extra coal because it would be impossible to find coal under a deep snowfall.

Sometimes in winter, kind railroad workers would shovel some loose coal over the sides of the coal cars as the train rumbled past Katie's neighborhood along the tracks. Who could tell how the coal accidentally landed beside the tracks behind the immigrants' shacks? But they could never depend on that happening. Railroad workers could be fined or even lose their jobs if they were caught sharing valuable coal for free.

If possible, Mama preferred being prepared without hoping for extra help. Being snowed in with plenty of coal in the house, and no reason to go out in the frigid weather, was a fine way to spend American Christmas Eve. This time, they were prepared.

Mama said they could hang their stockings tonight, but they would celebrate Russian Christmas on January 6 and 7 with a Christmas Eve feast and the midnight service at church. Katie was hopeful as she hung her stocking on the bedpost. She knew Mama couldn't pay Santa for a doll, but she couldn't stop wanting one. Once, she even prayed that God would send her a doll, but that felt selfish. God had more important things to do, so Katie tried not to pray about a doll anymore.

Her sisters each hung a stocking on the other bedposts, plus one for Ann in hopes that she would be able to come home from the Weises soon. Wasyl hung his stocking on the doorknob.

When the children were tucked in bed for the night, Mama sat in her rocking chair by the coal stove and led the children in softly singing Russian Christmas carols. One by one, the children drifted off to sleep until only Mama was left humming and rocking in the glow of the small oil lamp.

Early the next morning, Katie awoke to see several bulges in her stocking. Santa had come! What did he bring? she wondered. She shook Tillie and Mary, then ran over to Wasyl, "Santa came! He came!" she whispered so she wouldn't wake Mama.

The children scrambled to check the contents of their stockings. Each stocking held some walnuts in the shell, a square of chocolate candy, and a peppermint stick. Katie's stocking also held a pale blue hair ribbon and a pair of new black stockings. Tillie and Mary also got new black stockings and hair ribbons, red for Tillie and dark blue for Mary. In Wasyl's stocking was a new pair of black socks and a pair of warm winter gloves. In the very bottom of each stocking was an orange! Katie could barely remember last year's Christmas orange, but the thought of its juicy sweetness made her mouth water.

They didn't want to start before Mama woke up, so the girls began to quietly set the table for breakfast, while Wasyl let Prince outside and put fresh water in his bowl. Mary added a few pieces of fresh coal to the stove, and with the iron poker, she moved the glowing embers around to start the fire again. Katie slid the card she had made onto Mama's plate so that it would be the first thing she saw when she sat down. Mama was still sleeping, so they each peeled their own orange and waited in anticipation of this rare breakfast treat.

Prince's yelp and clattering reentrance as he charged through the kitchen door, and the children's squeals as he shook wet snow on them, finally woke Mama from her well-deserved sleep-in.

"Mama, Santa came! Look what he brought us!" Katie said, holding up her orange.

Mama smiled. "You all must have been very good this year." She picked up the Christmas card on her plate. "Who could this be from?" she asked.

"It's from me," said Katie. "See, I signed my name and printed 'Merry Christmas' all by myself."

"No, you didn't," corrected Wasyl. "The teacher wrote 'Merry Christmas' on the blackboard. You just copied it."

"Well, so did you!" Katie retorted as Wasyl held up his card to Mama.

"I added 'Happy New Year' to my card," he said. "How come you didn't?"

"It wouldn't fit," said Katie, noticing how large and crooked her printing looked next to Wasyl's.

"Children," said Mama, "let's have no arguing on this special day. I love both of your cards. Thank you, and Merry Christmas to you, too!"

Mary said, "Mama, I have a present for you, too. My present is…I got a job!" She grinned.

"A job? Where?" asked Mama.

"Mr. Kochuk hired me to wash spittoons in his saloon every morning. He will pay me, in cash money, ten cents each, and he said there would be four or five to wash each day. Will that help?"

"Yes," said Mama. "That will be a big help. You are smart, so I suppose six years is enough school for you?"

"It is," said Mary. "I already told my teacher that I wouldn't be returning after Christmas because I was needed at home. I want to earn money to help, just like Ann."

Tillie piped up, "That's not all, Mama. I can work, too. Nellie said that starting in the spring, Titka Catherine will let Mary and me bring their cows home from the field every day after school. She said Julia and Nellie are getting too old to do that chore, and she thinks proper young ladies shouldn't do that kind of work anyway. Titka Catherine said she will pay us a jug of milk every time! Merry Christmas, Mama!"

Mama hugged Mary and Tillie and said in Russian, "Oh, Marisha and Teklya, you are both growing up so fast, and I am very proud of my good big girls." Katie could see tears in Mama's eyes. She knew that her children's education was important to Mama. She also knew that Mama desperately needed help. She would never ask, but it was not unusual in the coal regions for children to quit school early so they could help financially support their family. Mary was smart and she was brave. Katie was sure that Mary was doing the right thing.

* * *

The rest of the day was relaxing and quiet. Outside, snow continued to fall until over twelve inches blanketed the ground by bedtime. Ann didn't come home, but Mama said she would probably come the next day if the weather cleared up. They planned a special dinner for the next day. Mama would make "bullets," the family's name for halushki—potato dumplings with cottage cheese, onions, and sauerkraut.

"No, no sauerkraut," begged Katie. "I hate sauerkraut. I don't want sauerkraut in mine."

"Hush!" said Mama. "It is a sin to complain about decent food. We must be thankful for every bite of food God gives us. I will make a small portion for you without sauerkraut, but next time just say, 'May I please have mine with no sauerkraut?' That is much better than complaining."

"Yes, Mama," said Katie. "Mama, may we open a jar of peaches tomorrow, too?" She remembered last summer when Mama **canned** all the peaches they could pick across the railroad tracks. Even though no one ever planted them, every kind of fruit tree grew beyond the tracks, because in that area the neighbors buried their garbage. So, any peach pits, plum pits, and fruit seeds in the mix grew and were naturally fertilized into a neighborhood orchard. Mama and the other ladies took advantage of it all.

"Of course," said Mama. "Aren't you glad we preserved all that fruit last summer? Now, even though the trees are bare and snow is on the ground, we have plenty of fruit to see us through the winter."

"And sauerkraut—don't forget, plenty of sauerkraut!" teased Wasyl, poking Katie in the side.

She knew this was a reference to Mama's big crock in the basement that seemed to have a bottomless supply of fermented cabbage. Ick, thought Katie, making a face. Sauerkraut!

## Chapter 11

December 26, 1914, was sunny and warm for the little Pennsylvania coal town. The deep blanket of accumulated snow had turned sooty gray and was melting into muddy puddles in the yards and alleys of the neighborhood by the tracks. Long, melting icicles dripped from the eaves of the houses. Occasionally, one would break loose and fall tinkling to the ground. Katie knew better than to stand under icicles.

Just as Mama predicted, Ann arrived that morning, and she had a tote bag full of surprises for everyone. For Mama, a lovely pair of pillowcases with a crocheted lace edging that Ann had made herself. Mama said, "Oh, Ann, I have never seen such fine work! When did you learn to crochet?"

Ann smiled. "All my girlfriends are crocheting now. Whenever we have free time." She shrugged. "It's the thing to do."

Tillie and Mary were each delighted to receive a thin metal crochet hook, a new linen handkerchief, and a little ball of colored thread. Ann promised to teach both girls how to crochet lace around their hankies that very day.

Wasyl's gift was a pocketknife. It wasn't new, but Ann had sharpened it on the whetstone in the Weises' kitchen, so it was just as sharp as new. Wasyl immediately brought in a twig from the yard and tried whittling as he had seen the boarders do when they sat around in the evenings. He was just practicing now, but once he learned how to handle the knife, he wanted to try carving a whistle that sounded different notes when you blew into it and moved your fingers over the holes.

Katie thought her gift was the best of all—a pair of roller skates just her size! Ann said the Weises' daughter had outgrown the skates, and Mrs. Weis told Ann that she could have them if they would fit one of her sisters. Katie was so happy she hugged her sister. "Thank you! Thank you! Thank you!" she said.

That wasn't all. Ann pulled out one last gift from the bottom of her bag. It was long and wrapped in butcher's paper—a big soup bone for Prince. What a treat! He loped over and sniffed it, wagged his tail, and then carried the treasure over to his spot near the coal stove, where he happily gnawed on his bone all afternoon.

Ann pulled the gifts from her own stocking and proceeded to peel and eat her orange as everyone tried to talk at once. The children told her all about their Christmas program at school. Tillie and Mary even recited their pieces for her.

"Will you sing 'Away in a Manger' for me?" Ann asked Katie and Wasyl, but Wasyl was too shy. Katie wasn't, though, so she sang all three verses by herself, and Ann clapped when she was finished.

Ann described Christmas at the Weises. She said that

even though they were Jewish, Mrs. Weis had decorated a tall Christmas tree in the parlor. The delicate glass ornaments and silver stars were imported from Germany and made the whole tree sparkle. When Mr. Weis had his managers in for their big holiday dinner, they even lit the tiny candles perched on the tree branches. Oh, it sounded so beautiful to Katie!

While Ann was teaching Mary and Tillie to crochet and Wasyl was whittling, Katie decided to try out her roller skates. She had never skated before, but she had watched other children skating on the sidewalk along Main Street. She had a fairly good idea of how to do it. These skates clamped on right over her shoes, and they had a special key to make them tighter or looser.

Carefully, Katie stood to her feet. Her skates started drifting forward, one to the right and one to the left. "Help!" she cried, but thud, she landed on the floor.

"Get up and try again," said Ann, so Katie scrambled to her knees and tried to pull herself up, but thud, she fell again…and again…and again. She was fighting tears now and just sat on the floor feeling sorry for herself.

"Oh, come on," said Wasyl, grabbing her hands and pulling her to her feet. "Now, just hold my hands and I'll take you around. Try to balance and stay on your feet."

Wasyl slowly walked backward through the kitchen, guiding her down the hallway to Mama's bedroom and back again. Katie held tightly to his hands. Her knees wobbled and her feet tried to go their own separate ways.

"Try moving your feet," said Wasyl. "If you lift one foot and then the other, you can put it down where you want to go."

Katie tried a few tottering steps. She still felt unsteady, but she was learning how to maintain her balance. Wasyl led her through the house several more times, and her confidence grew.

"Okay, I'm letting go now," he said.

"No!" cried Katie. "I can't!"

"Yes, you can. Just keep doing what you're doing now."

Katie took a few more steps and stopped rolling. "I stopped," she said. "Now what?"

"You have to push yourself forward with each step. Pump your legs," said Wasyl, demonstrating the movement her legs should make.

"Like this?" Katie tried to imitate her brother's instructions. Surprised, she began to move forward. She was doing it; Katie was skating! Then, thud.

This time, she pulled herself up and started again. Holding on to the wall for support, she was now skating all by herself. She practiced going up and down the hallway several times, but then decided to stop and rest. For some reason, she felt very tired, and her head and throat were beginning to hurt.

"Mama, I'm not really hungry for lunch. May I take a nap?" she asked.

"Of course," said Mama. Katie crawled onto the bed and pulled the quilt up to her chin.

* * *

That evening, Mama woke her for their special family dinner, but Katie said she still wasn't hungry, and she would rather sleep. Mama felt her head and frowned. "It feels warm," she said. Katie rolled over and continued to sleep.

Nighttime came. After everyone was in bed, Katie had a terrible nightmare. Something big and scary was chasing her, but in the dream, she was wearing roller skates and kept falling as she tried to get away. The something was getting closer and closer. Just as it reached out to grab her, she woke up screaming, "Mama! Mama!"

Mama hurried from her room, picked up Katie, and took her to the rocking chair. "It's just a dream, Little One," she murmured. "Just a dream." Katie's hair was damp with perspiration. She coughed long and hard and held her head. It hurt so much!

Mama tried to get Katie to drink some warm water and honey. "No, it hurts to swallow," said Katie.

"You must drink, Katie. You have a fever. Drinking liquids will help you to get well." Katie pushed the drink away.

Mama found a piece of flannel cloth and pinned it to the inside of Katie's petticoat to protect it from the Vicks VapoRub she was applying to Katie's chest. It would help to ease her congestion, but Katie just wanted Mama to stop fussing. Everything hurt—her head, her throat, her whole body ached. Mama tried to hold Katie in the rocking chair, but Katie was too hot. Mama laid her down on the bed and sat close by. Katie coughed again and began to shiver with chills.

* * *

By morning, both Mama and Katie were exhausted. Katie slept all the next day and night, while Mama offered occasional sips of sweetened water and warm broth. Mama said the garlic and salt in the broth would help Katie's throat feel better, but she didn't want to eat or drink anything. Katie just wanted to sleep. When she was sleeping, it didn't hurt so much.

Katie didn't even hear Ann leave early the following morning. By now, Mama was convinced that Katie had a bad case of the grippe. She was forcing Katie to take spoonfuls of water and broth every half hour or so just to keep her hydrated. Katie tossed and turned with feverish nightmares and tried to push Mama's hands away when she attempted to get Katie to drink something.

On the third day, Tillie woke up saying, "My throat hurts and my head, too." Mama got her to gargle with saltwater and drink some broth before rubbing her chest with Vicks. Mary moved into Mama's room, while Mama tended to the two sick sisters in the kitchen. Hopefully, Wasyl's cot was far enough away to avoid getting sick, too.

Katie's fever broke on the fourth day, but she was still coughing so much that her sides ached, and her head pounded. She did feel up to eating a few spoonfuls of soup and drinking a little water. She and Tillie slept fitfully most of that day and night.

It was two days later when Katie woke up feeling a little better. She asked for some toast. Mama made toast and coffee for her breakfast. "Mmm, that tastes good," said Katie. "I guess I was really hungry."

"That is a good sign. It means you are getting better," said Mama. "But look how thin you are! We will have to fatten you up before you return to school."

"Mama, what day is it?" asked Katie.

"It is December 31," Mama said. "New Year's Eve."

'No!" said Katie. "Did I miss it? December 28 I was supposed to go to Adeline's. Is it too late now?"

"I'm sorry, Little One. You were so sick you slept right through December 28. Don't worry. I told Ann to stop at Adeline's house on her way back uptown. They know you were sick, and that is why you couldn't visit."

"Thank you, Mama, but I really wanted to go to Adeline's. I missed seeing Aunt Gertrude, too."

"Well. I'm sure they are glad you didn't bring sickness to their house. When you are sick, it is always best to stay away from other people. Don't worry. There will be other opportunities to play at Adeline's when you are all better."

Tillie was still coughing and sleeping as much as she could. When Katie saw how flushed Tillie's face looked, with her red-rimmed eyes and matted hair, she wondered what she looked like after being sick for so long. She went to peek in the mirror over the sink. Her face looked so thin. Her bloodshot eyes had dark circles underneath, and her thin, mousey hair was tousled all over her head. She washed her face and combed her hair. There, that was better. At least she didn't have to look sickly. Food was starting to taste good again. Katie was on the mend.

## Chapter 12

The first day of school after Christmas vacation, Katie woke up to an empty house. Only Prince was there, peacefully sleeping in a spot of sunlight streaming in through the kitchen window. What? Where is everyone? She looked at the clock on the wall. 7:45 already! School starts at 8:30, and it's a long walk to get there! Why didn't anyone wake me? Why would they go to school without me? Where is Mama? Katie knew Mama certainly wouldn't allow her to sleep so late on a school day. She didn't smell any toast or coffee either. Didn't anyone make my breakfast today?

"Well, Prince, I guess it's up to me to get myself ready for school," she said to the only one listening. "I can do this."

Katie quickly washed her face and slipped her everyday dress over her head. She twisted, turned, and struggled until all the buttons were neatly buttoned down the back, but she couldn't find her bloomers. Mama had washed them yesterday, but when the weather was this cold, she usually brought damp clothes inside to finish drying overnight on the clothes rack by the stove. Today the clothes rack was empty and still folded up against the wall.

Katie cracked the kitchen door and saw her bloomers and the rest of Mama's laundry frozen stiff, still hanging on the clothesline. Now what am I supposed to do? She glanced at the clock. It was already eight o'clock. She had to think fast.

There's nothing I can do about bloomers. I can't wear them frozen solid. She decided to skip bloomers today and smoothed her dress down. She hoped no one would ever know. She combed her hair down and took a drink of water. No time for breakfast today. She pulled her boots on over her long black stockings, buttoned her coat, and tied her babushka under her chin. Less than twenty minutes before the school bell would ring. I will have to run!

Katie ran as fast as she could, her breath making little white puffs in the frosty air. It wasn't long before she got a stitch in her side and had to slow to a walk. She was feeling unsteady. I'm probably still a little weak from having the grippe, but I can't be marked tardy! Slowpokes got the paddle, and she didn't want that. She walked as fast as she could. Finally, she could see the school building ahead.

Just then, the school bell started ringing. A couple of stragglers were running up to the schoolyard as the other children began to line up according to grade in their assigned areas. Her feet felt heavy, but Katie pushed forward with all her might.

When she finally reached the schoolyard, Katie was feeling shaky and a little bit queasy. She stood for a moment gripping the iron fence, trying to catch her breath. Then she saw the line of first and second graders begin to file up the steps and into the building. They looked so far away. She tried to move toward that line, but suddenly the ground felt like it was shifting, and everything started to spin. Then it all went black.

* * *

Katie woke up on a cot in the teachers' lounge. Tillie was standing beside her, and Miss Wint was lightly slapping her cheek. "Katie, wake up! Can you hear me? Wake up, Katie!"

Katie groaned and opened her eyes.

"Oh, thank God," said Miss Wint. She offered Katie a drink of milk and some crackers. They tasted good after having no breakfast. "Katie, I want you to stay here and rest. At lunchtime, you may go home with Tillie and Wasyl, but I want you to stay there. You need to rest at home today." Katie nodded. "Tillie, you sit with Katie until lunchtime, okay?" With that, the teacher returned to her classroom.

"What happened?" asked Katie.

"You fainted in the schoolyard, that's what happened," said Tillie. "Miss Wint carried you into the school. You looked like you were dead!"

"I don't remember that," said Katie.

"And that's not all," continued Tillie. "When Miss Wint picked you up, your naked **dupa** was sticking right out in the open. Where are your bloomers?"

Katie gasped. "Did anyone see?"

"Well, I did. And I know Nellie did too, and she will never let you forget about that."

"Oh no," said Katie. She knew Tillie was right. If Nellie or Julia could find something to criticize about their cousins, they surely would. But it's not my fault! Everything went wrong this morning. "Why did you leave for school without me?" she asked Tillie. "No one woke me. No one made breakfast, and my bloomers were frozen on the line! Where is Mama?"

"Mama left for Breslau before sunrise. Titka Mary is very sick, so Mama is staying with her all day until Cousin Eustina gets home from work. Mama told us that you were staying home today because you still aren't well enough to go back to school. Mary went to take care of the cows, and Wasyl and I went to school. We tried not to wake you."

"Well, you should have! Nobody told me anything."

"You should have stayed at home until Mary came back. She would have explained everything. Maybe then Nellie wouldn't have seen your bare dupa," said Tillie.

"Maybe someone should have told me what was going on. It's not my fault!"

"Maybe you shouldn't be such a picky eater! Maybe then you wouldn't be so puny and sick for so long!"

"I am not such a picky eater! I eat everything I like," said Katie.

"The problem is that you don't like so many things.

You don't like eggs, you don't like chicken, you don't like sauerkraut, you don't like peas—did I miss anything?"

Katie's lower lip began to quiver. "Yes. Right now I don't like you!" She tried to hold back her tears. "You can just go back to your class, Tillie. I don't need you to sit here with me."

"Oh no," said Tillie, "I'm not getting into trouble because of you. I'm staying right here, just like Miss Wint said."

Katie turned toward the wall, exhausted, and fell asleep.

It seemed like no time at all before Tillie was shaking her shoulder. "Come on, Sleepyhead. Miss Wint said we should go home for lunch now." Katie sat up and blinked a few times. Then she remembered. How would she ever face the other students after what happened this morning?

The girls put on their coats, boots, and babushkas. Miss Wint had thoughtfully released them a few minutes early so they would have a head start for home, but it wasn't long before a stream of noisy students came running and skipping by on their way home for lunch. Then Katie heard it…

"I see London, I see France. Katie has no underpants!" It was Nellie, singing her taunt as she and a couple of her friends caught up to Katie and Tillie.

"Just ignore them," said Tillie, picking up the pace.

Katie bit her lip and kept walking.

"I see London, I see France. Katie has no underpants!" the girls behind them chanted.

Tillie grabbed Katie's hand and pulled her along. Katie

tried, but she couldn't walk any faster. The girls behind them kept teasing, whispering about some people being so poor they couldn't even afford underwear. Then again: "I see London, I see France. Katie has no underpants!"

Narrowing her eyes, Tillie planted her feet and jerked Katie to a stop. She whirled around and faced the three bullies. "Do you think you're funny?" she shouted. "Does it make you feel big to pick on a sick little girl? Maybe you should pick on someone your own size. How about me? Have anything to say to me?" Tillie's face was red, and her hands were balled into fists at her sides.

Nellie stepped up to Tillie until she was just a few inches from her face. "Yes," said Nellie. "It's too bad you're so poor that your little sister doesn't even have any under—"

Smack! Tillie punched Nellie in the face. Big drops of blood began to drip from Nellie's nose.

Katie gasped.

"Anyone else have anything to say?" asked Tillie as she glared at the other two girls.

"No, no," they mumbled. "We're just going home for lunch." They scurried on ahead of Katie, Tillie, and Nellie.

"You're going to be in big trouble! I'm telling my mother!" wailed Nellie.

"You just do that," said Tillie. "I'm telling my mother, too, and she is going to tell your father and maybe even the teacher! Then we'll see who's in trouble."

"Yeah, well..." began Nellie, sniffling and wiping the

blood dripping from her nose and chin.

"Leave my sister alone!" warned Tillie through clenched teeth. She turned, grabbed Katie's hand, and they walked toward home together.

"Are you really going to tell Mama?" Katie asked after a couple minutes.

"Oh, yes," said Tillie. "You know Nellie will tell. I just want Mama to hear the truth from us before she hears Nellie's version of what happened."

"Mama will be mad," said Katie.

"She will be, but not at us," said Tillie. "Not this time."

When they reached home, Mary had lunch waiting for them. Tillie told her the entire story about Katie fainting, no bloomers, and Nellie and her friends' cruel teasing.

"Ooo, that Nellie makes me so mad!" seethed Mary. "She would have never said anything if I were there with you. She knows that she would have to fight both of us then. She'd never risk that. Nellie is a typical bully, and I'm glad you taught her a lesson!"

"I would have hit her, too," Wasyl chimed in, "even if she is a girl. She's bigger than Katie, and that's just not right. Nellie better not let me hear her talking like that!"

"Calm down, Wasyl," cautioned Mary. "Mama will be upset enough to hear about this. You don't need to add anything else."

After Tillie and Wasyl returned to school, Katie tried to nap while Mary washed dishes and peeled the potatoes for supper this time. As Katie's thoughts bounced from frozen bloomers to fainting to Nellie's cruel comments and Tillie punching Nellie in the face, she just couldn't understand how this ordinary day had gone from bad to worse, and then to the worst day ever. The memory that disturbed her most was her telling Tillie that she didn't like her. Today, Tillie had been the best friend Katie had.

Now she worried about what would happen to Tillie. Her sister was in big trouble, and it was all because of Katie.

* * *

Mama entered the kitchen in a burst of cold air just as Mary was taking cabbage, potatoes, and sausage upstairs to the boarders' quarters. Tillie followed her with a tray of mugs and a fresh pot of hot coffee. Katie had set the kitchen table for the family's dinner of cabbage, potatoes, bread, and butter. Mama shut the door as quickly as possible so no warmth would escape. After removing her coat, boots, and babushka, she walked over to the stove to warm her hands and check on dinner.

She turned and looked around the room. Her tired smile told them she was pleased with what she saw. Soon everyone was seated around the table. Plates were passed to Mama, and she filled each plate and passed it back. No one spoke. No one looked directly at Mama. Serving herself last, Mama sat down, said a brief prayer of thanks for their food, and then they all began to eat... in silence.

After a few minutes, Mama put down her fork. "Maybe someone should tell me what happened here today," she said quietly. No one spoke. Katie looked at Tillie. Tillie looked at Katie. Mary cleared her throat, and Wasyl inspected the ceiling. "Well, I'm waiting," said Mama, more forcefully this time.

Katie bit her lip to keep from crying. Finally, she said, "It wasn't my fault. I mean, it was because of me, but nobody tells me anything. It's not fair!" She began to cry. "This was the"— sob—"worst day"—sob—"ever!"

Tillie rolled her eyes. "I did it. I punched Nellie in the face, and I'm glad I did it. She deserved it!"

Mama gasped. "Tillie, why would you do such a thing? That is terrible! I expect better behavior from you, Tillie!"

"Mama, Tillie is right. Nellie deserved it," said Wasyl.

"Were you there, Wasyl?" asked Mama.

"Well, no, but…"

"Then you be quiet. I want to hear what Katie and Tillie have to say."

Katie spoke first. "I woke up and nobody was here. I was late for school. I didn't know what to do. My bloomers were frozen on the line, and no one tells me anything!"

"We were quiet so we wouldn't wake her, just like you said, Mama," Tillie broke in. "Katie didn't know what to do, so she got dressed and ran to school so she wouldn't be late. Then she fainted, and Miss Wint carried her into the school, but Katie wasn't wearing bloomers. Her bare dupa was showing when the teacher picked her up. Some people saw it. Nellie saw."

"Tillie stayed with me until Miss Wint said we could go

home for lunch," said Katie. "That's when it happened."

"Nellie and her friends followed us," said Tillie. "They were teasing Katie. They said, 'I see London, I see France. Katie has no underpants!' Over and over—they just wouldn't stop. And they were saying other mean things like, 'You are so poor that you can't even afford underwear.'"

"We tried to ignore them," said Katie. "We tried to walk faster to get away from them, but they just walked faster, too."

Tillie continued, "Finally, I couldn't take it anymore. I turned around and told Nellie and her friends that they should pick on someone their own size, like me, instead of a sick little girl like Katie. Then Nellie got right in my face and said those same mean things again. I didn't even think, Mama. I don't know how it happened, but then my fist was in her face, and her nose was bleeding."

"Oh, dear," said Mama.

"Nellie said she was going to tell Titka Catherine. She will probably tell her a different story, but this is what really happened," said Tillie.

"That's right, Mama." Katie nodded fervently. "This is the truth."

Mama sat quietly, thinking. She looked around the table at each of her children. "I believe you," she said, "but this is going to cause a—"

A sharp knock at the door interrupted her.

The children sat wide-eyed as Mama went to answer it. As soon as she turned the knob, Titka Catherine stormed inside followed by Uncle Miron, hat in hand. Titka Catherine was waving Nellie's dress in front of Mama's face, pointing at the blood stains on the front.

"Your daughter did this," she said. "Tillie punched my poor Nellie in the nose for no reason at all, and we won't stand for this abuse from that wicked child. Isn't that right, Miron?" Prince was standing next to Mama now and growled a warning.

Uncle Miron still stood by the door, nervously twisting his hat in his hands. "Well, um, I think…" he began.

"We think Tillie should be switched so it doesn't happen again," interrupted his wife. "My poor Nellie is at home with an icepack on her red, swollen nose. It's probably broken, and her perfect profile will be ruined forever. Nellie cried like her heart was broken to think that her own cousin would attack her so viciously—and after all we've done for your family, too."

Prince continued to growl deep down in his throat.

"Catherine"—Uncle Miron put his hand on his wife's arm—"please calm down. You're scaring the children." He gestured at the stunned children seated around the table.

Katie put her face down on her folded arms, so she didn't have to watch.

"Why don't you both come in?" said Mama. "The coffee is hot. We can settle this calmly at the table."

She continued, "Children, finish your dinner, and then you may be excused to do your chores."

The children hurried to finish eating, then Mary and Tillie cleared the dishes and wiped the table. Mama placed two mugs and spoons on the table for Titka Catherine and Uncle Miron. Wasyl scraped dinner leftovers into Prince's dish and led him outside to eat on the porch. Katie, eyes downcast, got the broom and dustpan and began sweeping the floor.

Mama poured coffee into the adults' mugs and sat at the table facing Titka Catherine and Uncle Miron.

"Well, Anna," began Titka Catherine. "What are you going to do to Tillie so this will never happen again?"

"First of all," said Mama, "you should know that Katie has been terribly ill since before Christmas. She was in bed for days, not eating and delirious with fever. She should not have gone to school today at all."

"What does that have to do with Tillie's punishment?" snapped Mama's sister.

"Please, Catherine. We're sorry," said Uncle Miron. "We had no idea Katie was so ill."

"You probably have no idea that our sister, Mary, is also sick now, do you? I left early this morning to nurse her until Cousin Eustina could take over after work. I left instructions for the older children to allow Katie to stay home and sleep instead of going to school, but no one remembered to tell Katie. She woke up to an empty house, and—"

"And what about Tillie punching my Nellie in the nose?" demanded Titka Catherine.

"I'm getting to that," answered Mama. "Katie woke up to an empty house. She panicked, hurried to get dressed, and seeing her bloomers frozen on the clothesline, decided that no one would notice. So, she skipped breakfast and ran to school without any underpants. It was my fault. I should have explained everything to Katie before I left, but I was so worried about our sister. They think she has pneumonia."

"I'm still waiting to hear what all this has to do with my Nellie," said Titka Catherine, vigorously stirring sugar into her coffee.

"Katie arrived at school just as the bell rang, but because she was still so weak from her illness, she fainted in the schoolyard. When the teacher lifted her to carry her into the school, several students saw her bare dupa."

"That must have been embarrassing for her," said Titka Catherine.

"It was humiliating, especially since Nellie and her friends were among those who saw, and they decided to bully Katie about her misfortune. They followed Tillie and Katie at lunchtime, saying very mean things to them. My girls tried to ignore them. They tried to walk away, but—"

"I don't believe that!" interrupted Titka Catherine. "Nellie would never be so cruel! I want to hear the story straight from Tillie and Katie. Then we'll know who's lying. That just doesn't sound like our sweet Nellie, does it, Miron?"

"It sounds exactly like Nellie," said Uncle Miron. "There is no need for Tillie or Katie to say anything. I've told you before, Catherine, that you are too easy on our girls. I want them to have good manners and behave properly, but they have been getting away with too much. This time, I will be handling the discipline!"

"What?" Titka Catherine gasped in surprise.

Uncle Miron slammed his fist so hard on the table that coffee splashed out of his mug. He rose and said, "Come on, Catherine. We're done here!"

Titka Catherine, suddenly silent, got up and followed her husband to the door.

"Anna, I'm sorry we have bothered you. You won't mind if I cut a switch from your peach tree now, will you?" asked Uncle Miron.

"Not at all," said Mama.

"I apologize for our daughter's bad behavior, and I'm embarrassed by the shame she has brought on our family. She will be disciplined."

"But—but Miron…" stammered Titka Catherine.

"Come along, Catherine," he said, nudging her out the door. With a slight bow, he closed the door behind him.

Everyone stood silent and shocked, then… "That was great!" whispered Tillie.

"Not so fast." Mama gave her a stern look. "The only reason you aren't in trouble, Tillie, is because you were defending your little sister against a bully. That is right, but you must learn to control your temper in situations like that. Often when you hit someone else, they fight back. So, try to think first. You must be willing to accept the consequences of your actions. In addition, if I ever hear that you are the one who started a fight for any reason, then you will be in much more trouble than Nellie is right now." Mama looked around the room at each child.

"Does everyone understand?"

"Yes, Mama," they all answered.

## Chapter 13

January 6 is a very special day. It is Ukrainian Christmas Eve according to the **Julian calendar**. Katie was happy that her family celebrated both Christmases. Ukrainian Christmas is a bit different from American Christmas. Ukrainian Christmas is all about the birth of Jesus, and everything that day has a special significance in the story of the Nativity.

For Holy Evening (Christmas Eve), Mama was preparing a special dinner that included twelve traditional dishes, representing the twelve disciples of Christ. Everyone would be expected to eat a little bit of each meatless and dairy-free dish, even if they didn't like it. Only meatless and dairy-free foods were served at this dinner, in honor of the kind animals who shared their stable with baby Jesus on the first Christmas Eve. For their dinner, Mama was preparing pierogies, mushrooms, **borscht**, sauerkraut cooked with onions and barley, peas, meatless **holobchi**, pickled herring, stewed apples and prunes, and a fish. Some families had salmon, but Mama was preparing a carp instead, which was much less expensive. Kolach, a special Christmas bread, was always on the table representing Christ, who is called the Bread of Life.

The entire day was a fast day—no eating solid food until the first star appeared in the sky. Mama explained that the reason they waited for the first star to appear was in remembrance of the three kings who followed the star to Bethlehem. Katie and Wasyl stood vigil at the window, watching the sky for a sparkle of starlight.

Meanwhile, the older girls set the table with a white tablecloth, signifying the purity of Jesus, the spotless Lamb of God. A candle in the middle of the table represented Jesus, the Light of the World. Straw spread around the base of the candlestick stood for the hay in the manger where baby Jesus slept.

Katie was really getting hungry now. She hoped they would see a star soon.

"I'm going outside to watch for the star," said Wasyl.

"It has to be dark before you can see a star," said Mary. "It's only four o'clock in the afternoon."

"Well, I don't want to miss it," he answered, buttoning his coat and pulling on his gloves. Katie preferred to watch the sky from inside, where it was warm and smelled so delicious.

Mary and Tillie remembered to set an extra place at the table for "The Uninvited Guest," and they placed a candle in the window to welcome any homeless person or person who had no family, who might want to join them. Mama said that you should never refuse to feed anyone who came to your door on Christmas Eve, because it might be the Christ Child in disguise; you never knew. It could happen.

Suddenly, Wasyl burst through the kitchen door carrying a big box with "KATIE" printed on it. "Katie, look what I found on the steps! It's for you!" he said.

"For me? What could it be?" Katie rushed over to the box and stared at it in wonder.

"Well, don't just look at it, Onion Eyes—open it and see what's inside!"

"Okay," said Katie. She tried to get the string off, but it was tied too tightly. Wasyl took his knife out of his pocket and sliced through the strings holding the box shut. Mama and the girls gathered around to see what could be inside.

Katie gasped. A doll... It was a doll! She had long brown hair and a red dress. Katie lifted her from the box and noticed the doll's eyes flutter open. "Ma-ma," cried the doll. Katie began to cry. She cried, and she couldn't stop. "She's just what I wanted," Katie sobbed.

"There's a note inside," said Mary. "Do you want me to read it?"

Katie wiped her tears with the back of her hand. "Yes, please."

"It says, 'Dear Katie, when I saw this doll, I thought of you. I hope you like her. Love, Aunt Gertrude.'"

"And look," said Tillie. "There's something more in the box." She lifted out a jigsaw puzzle and a box of dominos. There was another note, too. Tillie read, "'Here are some games for you and your family to play together on cold winter nights.'"

"Oh, Mama, that was so nice of Aunt Gertrude!"

"Yes." Mama smiled. "She is a truly kind lady."

Katie wouldn't put her doll down. She hugged her and walked around the room thinking for a while before saying, "I think I will name her Rose, because she has a tiny rose in her hair." She carried Rose over to the window to watch for the first star—and there it was! Wasyl confirmed that he could see the star, too. It was finally time to eat!

Katie ate a little bit of everything. She didn't even complain about the sauerkraut. She couldn't help smiling. All she could think about was how happy she was to have Rose, a doll of her very own.

When dinner was finished, they sang Ukrainian Christmas carols around the table. After that, it was time for a short nap before heading to church for midnight mass.

"Mama, may I take Rose to church?" asked Katie.

"No, that would not be a good idea," said Mama. "Other little girls might see your doll and be sad that they don't have a doll. Remember how you used to feel? It is not kind to show off what you have in front of others." Katie hadn't thought of that. "Rose can sleep on your bed until we get home."

"Okay," said Katie, and she laid Rose on the bed and covered her to stay warm until she returned.

The dim streetlights cast shadows and the wind blew cold as they trudged to the church, but other families were also making their way through the slumbering town. It was a quiet, friendly pilgrimage. The service was long, but beautiful in the glowing, candle-lit church, incense wafting through the sanctuary. Mama said the incense carried their prayers up to heaven.

One by one, the people filed to the front to take the blessed bread and wine, symbolic of the body and blood of Christ. When the congregation sang carols, Katie tried to stay awake, but she soon fell asleep against Mama's arm. The music sounded like a lullaby.

It wasn't long before Mama was gently nudging Katie awake for the chilly walk home.

\* \* \*

Everyone slept late the next morning. Ukrainian Christmas Day is a holy day, so no unnecessary work is done. They ate meals of leftovers from the night before and celebrated a day of rest. Katie was quietly rocking Rose, but she was thinking about last night.

"Mama," said Katie, "when I thought Santa couldn't bring me a doll, I prayed and asked God to send me one. Then I thought that was a selfish prayer, and I still do, but do you think God sent me my doll? Even if it was a selfish prayer? Or was it because I was good, like Santa gives presents if you're good? I think God answered my doll prayer. Do you?"

Mama was silent for a long time, and Katie thought she might not answer. Then she said, "Katie, God is not like Santa Clause. God loves us. You don't have to earn His gifts. He doesn't grant our every wish, but God is love.

Sometimes he does something special just because he wants to make us happy. I have noticed that God usually uses people to do His work. He could have made your doll miraculously appear in an instant, but God used Aunt Gertrude to do it instead. That is why we must always listen for what He is telling us to do, because God may want you to do something special for someone else."

"I've never heard God talk to me. How can I hear Him?" Katie asked.

"To hear God, you don't listen with your ears. You listen with your heart," said Mama. "When you have a strong feeling that you should do something kind for someone else, that's God. He is always love, but He uses people to show that love to others."

"Aunt Gertrude didn't even know that I prayed for a doll," said Katie.

"But God did. He whispered that thought to Aunt Gertrude, and she obeyed Him."

"Mary said she would help me write a thank-you note to Aunt Gertrude," said Katie. "I want to write one to God, too."

Mama stroked Katie's hair and said, "Katie, God is always near, and He is always listening. You can thank Him right now if you want."

Katie was quiet for a few minutes.

"Katie, what are you thinking now?" asked Mama.

"Oh, I'm not thinking," said Katie, her eyes closed tight. "I'm thanking God."

## Chapter 14

Spring was struggling to wrestle herself from winter's grip this year. One sunny day was followed by two chilly days of pelting rain. Mama occasionally walked down to survey the river. So far, the Susquehanna was behaving. Runoff water was constantly trickling down the steep slopes on both sides of the river, and the cold, gray water was rushing by faster and deeper than usual. Flooding was always a concern for everyone in Katie's neighborhood, but despite the snow melt causing muddy puddles and mushy backyards, at least the powerful river was staying within its banks. It would not flood their little neighborhood this year.

The promise of spring meant planting on The Flats would commence in just a couple of weeks. Mama would soon be able to return to work. With that in mind, Mama was determined to spring clean the entire house before then.

Living so close to the mines and railroad tracks caused a layer of fine coal dust to coat everything most of the year. Scrubbing the soot away was a fact of life. But, as Mama always said, "Soap and water are cheap, so there's no excuse for being dirty." Mama wouldn't feel right about starting back to work unless the house was spotless before then.

This sunny Saturday, Ann was home to help them. She gathered the bedding from all the beds, including the boarders,' and took them out to the yard where Mama had placed three washtubs under the bare grape arbor. The first tub was filled with scalding hot water that Wasyl had carried in buckets from the **engine house**. Mama let a few pieces of bedding soak for a while, swishing and stirring them with a long wooden poker, until the water cooled enough for her hands to rub each article with lye soap and scrub them on the **scrubbing board**. When Mama was satisfied that each piece was clean, she would wring it out by hand and rinse out all remaining soap in the second and third tubs, which were filled with cold water. Finally, everything was wrung out one last time and deposited in the wicker clothes basket standing nearby.

Wasyl's job, besides running back and forth to the engine house for hot water, was to beat all the rag rugs. First, he shook out all the loose dirt over the porch railing. Then he draped each rug over an empty clothesline far away from Mama's clean laundry and beat the remaining dirt out with a **rug beater**. It was dusty work, but he made it a game, pretending he was thrashing "the bad guys" he had captured.

Mary and Tillie were washing walls and windows indoors. It made Katie feel a little guilty knowing how many times she had smudged those windows, fogging them with her breath and then drawing on the glass with her fingers. The evidence of her artwork stretched as far up on each window as she could reach.

Katie was the smallest, so her job was to scrub the floors on her hands and knees. Mama's wood floors were bleached almost white from years of scrubbing. The boarders often said, "Mrs. Swistovich keeps such a clean house you could eat off the floors." Really? thought Katie. Who would do that? But she understood that the floors had better be spotless when she was finished with her job.

Katie had a bucket of soapy water and a scrub brush to loosen the dirt, and another bucket filled with clear water and a rag for rinsing the soap and dirt away. The older children helped move the furniture so Katie could get into all the corners and under the table and beds. When she needed more clean water, Wasyl would run to fetch more, and refilled both buckets for her. It took a long time, but she did the entire first floor of the house, and then called Mama in to inspect it.

Mama removed her shoes on the porch, and then came in to examine the girls' work. She was pleased with what they had accomplished on the first floor and said they could all break for lunch now. They sat on the back porch to eat their sliced **kielbasa** sandwiches and rest.

After lunch, Mama dispatched Mary and Tillie to help Ann upstairs. The boarders had been given strict orders to vacate the premises today, and Mama wanted the men's living area to be completely clean before they returned that evening.

"What should I do now?" asked Katie.

"You may clean the porches," said Mama. "Sweep them with the broom first, and then scrub and rinse them just as you did the floor inside."

"Okay," said Katie. As she swept, she devised a plan.

She grabbed two strong rubber bands from the kitchen drawer and used them to attach one scrub brush to each foot. Then she sloshed some soapy water onto the back porch and began to skate around on the scrub brushes. This is fun, she thought, smiling to herself.

Up and down the length of the porch she skated, making sure to poke the scrub brushes into all the corners as she skated around on the rough wooden boards. This was harder than skating on roller skates, but much more fun than scrubbing on her hands and knees. When Katie was satisfied that she had loosened as much dirt as possible, she poured clean water over the soapy mess and skated to the edges to watch the dirty water cascade off the porch. She didn't notice Mama standing at the bottom of the steps until she heard a chuckle.

Mama said, "It looks like you've found a way to make work fun. Good girl!"

"I'm going to do the front porch next," said Katie. "This doesn't feel like work at all!"

Wasyl helped Katie carry two buckets of clean water to the front porch and then went to see who else was ready for more water. Katie again used the rubber bands to attach the scrub brushes to her shoes and proceeded to skate around the soapy porch. Before long, she had attracted an audience.

Of course, Frankie Leskovich was the first to walk over and gawk as Katie skated back and forth. She even added a slightly ungraceful pirouette turn to make him giggle. Lina Vengloski, who lived two houses past Frankie's, arrived to take the little boy back to his own yard, but she stayed to watch, too. Finally realizing that her son was no longer playing in their yard, Mrs. Leskovich showed up looking for Frankie. Everyone stood watching Katie's new technique for washing the porch.

"I could do that," said Frankie softly.

"What did you say?" asked his mother, her eyes widening in surprise. Frankie hardly ever spoke.

"I could do that," he said, pointing at Katie's feet.

"Really? Well, let's go find out," said Mrs. Leskovich, smiling. She put an arm around Frankie's thin shoulders and led him back home to find two scrub brushes, two rubber bands and a bucket of water.

Lina Vengloski stayed. "May I try that?" she asked.

"If you can get two scrub brushes and two rubber bands from home, we can skate together," said Katie.

"Okay, I'll be right back!"

It didn't take long for Lina to return. She and Katie skated, slipping and sliding around the front porch, squealing and giggling the whole time.

"My mother says we must do our porch next," said Lina.

All right! Katie had a new friend!

## Chapter 15

Mama was now working full-time on The Flats. The days were getting longer and warmer—perfect weather for farming the fertile lowlands along the river. The fruit trees in the yard and across the tracks wore beautiful pink and white blossoms. In Mama's backyard garden, rows of bright green sprouts promised a bountiful crop of onions, peas, beans, cabbage, tomatoes, and squash. Everyone helped with the garden, even though Mama had assigned Wasyl that particular job, because the family would have to live all year on whatever their garden produced during the summer. Gardening was important work.

Wasyl had to bury the kitchen vegetable peelings in the garden and spread coal ashes around the tomato plants to fertilize the soil. He had to pull the stubborn weeds so they wouldn't compete with the vegetable seedlings for water and nourishment. Everyone was on the lookout for insects that might damage healthy young plants. Wasyl put a jar of water in the corner of the garden. When anyone saw an insect invader attacking the plants, they pinched the offender off and dropped it into the jar of water. Several times a week, Wasyl carried the jar of drowned bugs across the railroad tracks and dumped them there. Even the chickens helped keep the garden insect-free and fertilized as they wandered and pecked around the young plants.

Ann continued living and working at the Weises, and Mary's job of washing spittoons at Mr. Kochuck's saloon had expanded to include general cleaning of his establishment and more pay. He said Mary was "a very dependable worker." She showed up on time each morning and worked until noon every day except Sunday, when the saloon was closed. Ann and Mary were proud to give their pay to Mama to help support the family.

Tillie took Titka Catherine's cows out to the field every morning, and she and Mary brought them in each evening. Tillie was proud to see Mama's smile when they brought home the promised jug of warm milk each night. Even though it wasn't cash money, it was an important contribution to the family.

Of course, picking coal was a never-ending chore. Although the days were warmer, the coal stove still had to be kept going, and it was never too soon to start piling up a good supply for next winter. You could never have too much coal.

Lina Vengloski and Katie walked to school together every day now. When Adeline came after school to help peel potatoes, Katie and Lina walked her home in time for dinner. The schoolyear would be ending soon, and Katie didn't know how often she would be able to see Adeline during the summer. She was glad that Lina lived close by, but a whole summer was a terribly long time. She would miss Adeline.

Adeline was worried, too. She didn't want to spend every summer day alone in the apartment while her parents worked in their tavern. Adeline dreaded playing alone with only her toys for company. The girls were trying to think of a plan to get together during summer vacation. What could they do?

Katie and Adeline thought and thought, and talked about what they thought, but they still couldn't come up with a plan. Finally, it was the last week of school.

"Adeline, maybe we should ask our mothers to help us with a plan," said Katie one day at recess.

"I will talk to my mother tonight," said Adeline.

"Me, too," agreed Katie.

* * *

"Mama, I'm so glad that Lina lives near us so we can play together this summer," began Katie.

"As long as you don't neglect your chores," reminded Mama.

"Yes," said Katie. "Work first, then play. But Mama, I will miss Adeline if I can't see her at all this summer. Adeline is my very best friend. She will miss me, too. We don't know what to do. Can you help?"

Mama slowly shook her head. "I am sorry, but I can't help. Working all day and taking care of the house and the boarders leaves me no time for trips uptown. And don't even think about asking your sisters. They will be too busy with their own jobs. Maybe Adeline's mother can help."

"That's okay," Katie said softly, her face falling. "I just thought I'd ask."

The next day at recess, Adeline reported that her mother had said the same thing. "She said that working in the tavern and keeping house was all she could handle," said Adeline. "That means I'll have no one to play with all summer."

"I just don't know what to do," said Katie, blinking back tears.

"Do about what?" asked Lina, skipping up to her two friends.

"Getting together with Adeline this summer. Both our mothers say they're too busy to help. Do you have any ideas, Lina?"

"Hmm, I will have to talk to my mother tonight," said Lina. "I think I might have a plan…if it works."

Katie and Adeline smiled hopefully. Maybe Lina's mother could help.

* * *

Before school the next morning, Lina ran to Katie's house and knocked rapidly on the back door. Panting, she pulled Katie outside and whispered, "It worked! I talked to my mother, and she talked to my uncle, and he said it's all right with him if it's all right with your mother and Adeline's." She stopped to catch her breath. "So, you have to get them both to agree, and then he'll do it!"

"Do what?" asked Katie.

"My Uncle Herman is the Umbrella Man. He said he would help!"

"You mean the man who drives his horse and wagon up and down the streets crying 'Oom-bar-ella! Oom-bar-ella!' is your uncle?"

"Yes! He's my mother's brother. Mondays and Wednesdays, he drives around town calling for broken umbrellas and delivering the ones he has already repaired. He could bring Adeline down to visit us on one of those days and even take her back home again. He's busy working uptown in his shop the rest of the week, but he said that on those days it would be no trouble at all to pick up Adeline in the morning and drop her off at home in the evening. He passes right by her house anyway."

"Oh, Lina, that's a great idea! I can't wait to tell Adeline!" Katie could barely contain her joy. "We can ask our mothers tonight. Let's hurry now so we're not late for school!"

That evening, Katie waited until Mama was done with dinner and the children's chores were completed before she approached Mama.

"Mama, did you know that Lina's uncle is the Umbrella Man?"

"No, I didn't know that," said Mama as she bustled around the kitchen preparing for the next day.

"He is. He drives his wagon around town on Mondays and Wednesdays calling for broken umbrellas, and he said that he would bring Adeline to visit us on those days.

He will even take her home again—that is, if you say it's okay. Please?" said Katie.

"I don't know." Mama frowned. "Having Adeline here all day might interfere with your chores, and it does seem like a great inconvenience for Lina's uncle Herman. Are you sure he agreed to this plan?"

"He says he passes right by Adeline's house, so it's no trouble for him to pick her up in the morning and take her home at the end of the afternoon," said Katie. It's only Mondays and Wednesdays, but it's better than not seeing each other all summer. Please, Mama?"

"I will have to think about this," said Mama.

Katie knew the subject was closed until Mama made up her mind, but the word "chores" brought another thought to her mind.

"Mama, everyone has a job to do this summer, except me. What can I do? I want to help, too."

Mama smiled. "I forget you are getting to be a big girl now—almost in second grade. There must be some little thing you can do to help me this summer."

"But, Mama, I don't want to do a little thing. I want to do something big and important to help," said Katie.

"Big and important," said Mama. "Hmm. I know…you can peel the potatoes."

"Peel potatoes? But I do that all the time," protested Katie. "That's not a big, important job."

"Oh, but peeling potatoes is a very important job, Katie. How could I cook potatoes if you didn't peel them? What would we eat? The boarders wouldn't even want to live here if I didn't serve potatoes, and we would lose all that income. If you didn't peel potatoes, we would have no peelings to feed our garden, and then the plants would grow weak and scrawny. We would have a poor harvest and nothing to can for winter."

Katie's pale green eyes grew wide. Her family might starve? The boarders would leave? Everyone was depending on Katie to peel potatoes. That is a big, important job!

"Oh, Mama, I never knew that peeling potatoes is so important. I will peel as many potatoes as you want!"

"Of course, that will mean coming in from play by three o'clock every day to start peeling, even when Adeline is visiting…no excuses."

"Yes, Mama, and Adeline will help!" Katie clapped her hands and jumped up and down. Mama agreed!

"And I will expect all the eyes and bad spots to be removed from the potatoes. You must promise to do this big important job correctly, just as you would if I were standing next to you watching."

"I will do my best all summer. You can count on me," said Katie.

"I know I can." Mama smiled. She wrapped her arms around Katie's thin shoulders. "I know I can."

Katie sighed and relaxed in Mama's hug. It was going to be a great summer!

If you have enjoyed reading
"Peeling Potatoes: Katie's Story", please
leave a review on Amazon letting me
know what you thought of the book.
Thanks so much!

To follow the author and receive news
about upcoming books in the
"Rocked in the Cradle of Coal Series", visit
jaynembooth.com

# Glossary

**Babushka:** A triangular headscarf worn by eastern European peasant women and girls. It is traditionally tied under the chin. Babushka is also the word for grandmother or old lady in Russian, Ukrainian, and Polish.

**Borscht:** Red beet soup. Mama made it with no meat and served it with sour cream.

**Canned (to can, v):** A common method of preserving vegetables and fruit that involves placing prepared food in sterilized glass jars with rubber ringed lids and heat processing the jars in boiling water to seal them. Properly canned food is shelf stable for months at room temperature.

**Culm:** Steep hills of low-quality coal and shale discarded by the mining companies and piled in huge mounds around the coal mines and breakers of the anthracite region in Northeastern Pennsylvania.

**Chrusciki:** (pronunciation: hrrooss-CHEE-kee), "or angel wings" A simple flaky pastry treat, deep-fried in lard, and showered in powdered sugar.

**Dupa:** A Polish/Ukrainian slang word for a person's backside or rear end.

**Engine house:** This structure serviced the steam trains that carried coal from the mines to points of delivery. At the engine house, water was preheated to get the trains quickly up and running after repairs.

**The Flats:** Level low-lying land along the Susquehanna River. The Flats were very fertile from years of deposited silt during seasonal flooding. This area was perfect for farming. (Also known as The Shawnee Flats in Plymouth, PA.)

**Grippe:** An old-fashioned term for influenza, "the grippe."

**Halushki:** A traditional and economical comfort food that comes from Central and Eastern Europe. It consists of fried onions and cabbage with thick homemade noodles or small dumplings. Variations can include cottage cheese, sauerkraut instead of cabbage, or kielbasa.

**Holobchi:** (Also Halupki, Holubky, or Golumpki) An eastern European dish consisting of stuffed cabbage rolls normally filled with a beef and/or pork and rice mixture wrapped in a steamed cabbage leaf and covered in a sweet tomato sauce.

**Julian Calendar:** The Julian calendar was created under Julius Caesar in 45 BC. The Russian, Greek, and other Eastern Orthodox churches still follow it to calculate religious holidays even though most of the world follows the Gregorian calendar proposed by Pope Gregory of Rome in 1582. Russian Christmas is celebrated on January 7, according to the Julian Calendar.

**Kielbasa:** A Polish smoked and highly seasoned pork or pork and beef sausage.

**Old Country:** This was the term used by any early immigrant to signify the country of his birth…wherever he lived before coming to America.

**Piece:** A poem or portion of prose memorized to recite.

**Pierogies:** Pasta dumpling filled with mashed potatoes and cheese, onions, sauerkraut, or fruit. Pierogies are a popular peasant dish brought to America by immigrants from Central and Eastern Europe.

**Titka:** Ukrainian word for Aunt.

**Primer:** The elementary school reading book used by young schoolchildren. Katie's class read from the first-grade primer.

**Rug beater:** Before the vacuum cleaner, rug beaters were the common tool used to beat dust and dirt out of carpets. They had a long handle with a looped or woven wire or rattan paddle at the end.

**Scrubbing board:** A rectangular board or frame with a corrugated metal surface on which clothes are rubbed in the process of handwashing; also called a wash board.

## About the Author

Jayne M Booth was born in, and spent her childhood in, Northeastern Pennsylvania. As a second-generation American descended from miners in an area still sprinkled with the skeletal remains of coal breakers and reclaimed **culm** banks, she has heard these stories echoed from family, friends, and neighbors. Everyone in her childhood knew someone who worked for the mines, lost their life in the mines or from Black Lung Disease, or had even experienced a cave-in – maybe even in their backyard! Someone had to write the stories!

Determined to preserve the mining experience as seen through the eyes of the children, she interviewed those who lived through it and wrote down what they shared. She hopes to provide a glimpse back into history, into the lives of the poorest of the poor, the nobility of honest hard work, and the progression of each generation of the American experience achieving a bit more than the previous one. There are lessons there for all of us.

Jayne is the mother of four and the grandmother of three. She resides in Maryland with her husband and little dog, Pepper, her motivation for stepping away from the keyboard and getting out in the sunshine every day.

More books in the Rocked in the Cradle of Coal Series are coming. To follow Jayne and stay updated, please visit her website, jaynembooth.com.

Made in the USA
Coppell, TX
20 August 2022